M000198190

*This book should be required reading in every school system as a model of how to find your talent, a belief in oneself without falling victim to the downward, dismal spiral that can come from growing up in a dysfunctional atmosphere.*

~ Paul Atreides,
*Las Vegas Review-Journal*

*IA: Initiate is a great read from start to finish. John Winston does a masterful job of capturing the hearts of his characters, making them feel real, and in doing so he captures the hearts of his readers.*

~ Allison Maruska,
Author of *The Fourth Descendant* and
The Project Renovatio Trilogy

*IA: Initiate has the potential of becoming a new literary phenomenon.*

~ Bil Howard, Readers' Favorite

JOHN DARRYL WINSTON
PRESENTS

# IA
# INITIATE
### AN IA NOVEL, BOOK ONE

H2O

LIVONIA, MICHIGAN

Book design by Blue Harvest Creative
www.blueharvestcreative.com

## IA: INITIATE

Published by H2O
an imprint of BHC Press

Library of Congress Control Number:
2016962382

ISBN-13: 978-1-946006-36-3
ISBN-10: 1-9460-0636-X
Also available in Hardcover & eBook

Visit the author at:
www.johndarrylwinston.com &
www.bhcpress.com

# ACKNOWLEDGMENTS

Dominique Wilson

For Marquette, the real Meridian and
John, the greatest musical artist
the world has never known

# TABLE OF CONTENTS

## PART ONE: BEGINNING

## PART TWO: DURATION

# PART THREE: DISSOLUTION

# FUN AND GAMES

in·i·ti·ate [v. ih-**nish**-ee-eyt]

1. to cause something,
especially an important event
or process to begin

# PART ONE
# BEGINNING

IN THE PAST...

A n auditorium is filled with admirers who are anxiously waiting to hear the cutting-edge theories of leading scientist, Dr.
Cornelius Andersen. The brilliant young scientist in a striking black
tuxedo and hair wild atop his head is waiting backstage in the auditorium for his introduction. With him is his beautiful wife, Camille,
in an elegant, lavender gown. The air is electric this evening. Rumor
has it that Dr. Andersen will shock the scientific community with
an announcement of groundbreaking discovery.

"So, you still think this is a bad idea, honey?" asks Cornelius.

"You don't even have to ask. You know how I feel," says Camille,
shaking her head.

"Now watch this. Wasn't it you who always told me that if I
went with my heart, then it was the right thing to do?"

"I know. But sometimes it's not always about right or wrong,
Cory. Sometimes it's about having a good reason." She puts her
hand on her stomach acknowledging her unborn child and looks at

him. "And this, your family, should be good enough reason for you to let it go."

He smiles and places his hand on top of hers. "But don't you see? That's just it. This is for us, all of us. It's for you and me ... and him," he says, looking at her stomach. "Things are changing all around us, Cam, and not for the better. You know that. These discoveries will not only change the world, but they will also give our son an advantage—abilities we can only dream of. He will be a king among men, even more."

"It just doesn't seem right. Why can't he ... why can't we, just be normal, like everybody else?"

"Because to the normal—the average everyday folk—freedom is an illusion." Seemingly from nowhere, he produces a shiny brass, odd-shaped skeleton key, as if he has pulled it from the sky. "Something to be divvied up by the ones in power, the ones who stand above, at the whim of others." He makes a throwing motion upward, the key disappears into thin air, and fine, silver dust appears in its place. "But for those of us who know where our real power resides, for those of us who have the courage to challenge those powers and the will to do what is necessary, we will possess the key to unlock the door to any desire imaginable ... the only true freedom." He slowly pulls her hand away from her stomach to reveal the shiny brass key that is now resting in her palm. She smiles and closes her hand around it.

"Are you ready, Dr. Andersen?" asks the Master of Ceremonies, as he startles Camille by approaching the couple from behind.

"I am, sir," replies Cory confidently.

"And let me say that I am honored to have the opportunity to meet you and introduce you all in one night," the man adds.

"*Merci beaucoup,*" replies Cory.

As the Master of Ceremonies makes his way to the podium, the murmuring from the audience dwindles to silence.

"Oh, Cory," says Camille, trembling.

"Trust me," reassures Cory with a confident smile on his face.

"Ladies and gentlemen," the Master of Ceremonies begins. "I stand before you in awe. I've just had the pleasure of meeting the person I am about to introduce to you this evening. He is a person who truly needs no introduction. He is an alumnus and adjunct professor of particle physics at our own Harvard University. He received his Ph.D. from Cambridge University. He is a recipient of the Copley Medal, the oldest and most prestigious award given by the Royal Society of London. He has recently been awarded the J.J. Sakuri Prize for Theoretical Particle Physics."

"You didn't tell me about that one," says Camille, her eyes wide.

"First I've heard of it," replies Cory with a raised eyebrow.

"Last year he applied a new complex mathematical model created from Albert Einstein's General Theory of Relativity," continued the Master of Ceremonies. "And he is the youngest scientist ever to receive a Nobel Prize in Physics. I give you, Dr. Cornelius Andersen."

The entire audience—scientists, mathematicians, alumni, students, faculty, and reps from the media—rises and gives thunderous applause as Cory makes his way to the podium.

# 01: THE EXCLAVE

## PRESENT DAY...

It is the city, a city that never dies although some of its inhabitants meet that fate daily. The city lives and breathes day and night, dark or light. In contrast to the city's downtown with its skyscrapers, arenas, and casinos, the northern neighborhoods are like a sea of identical blocks attached to a grid of intersecting lines. Suburbanites pass through the city into its downtown and then return to their perfect palaces. This image from high above suggests a pattern of order that is betrayed by the chaos found below where uncertainty is the only certainty and chaos the only order. This chaos is reverently referred to with pride by its indigenous population as the Exclave.

Smoke and its accompanying aromas fill the hot, humid air on this early, late summer morning. There is smoke from late night and early morning cooking, smoke from all manner of narcotics, and smoke from smoldering house fires set and put out through the night—although some are still ablaze.

And there are the sounds that set this scene: a dog barking relentlessly, sporadic gunfire, sirens in the distance, a train that passes through like clockwork, and a constant beat and rhythm coming from somewhere … everywhere … nowhere, that define the "silence" of the Exclave at dawn.

It is feared by those who are on the outside and rightly so. But it is home to those inside its invisible walls. Like a modern-day Troy, it is safe haven for some; however, for others, it is a place from which there is no escape. But there are a few that see bigger things and different places—other worlds.

## 02: NAZ

One such young man, a thirteen-year-old, living in Marshal Park, Section 31, on the corner of Wessen and Smith, is stirring as our story begins. He has actually been awake for a while now, drifting and rolling with each familiar and unfamiliar sound as a fighter would roll with each punch. He couldn't recall ever boxing before but remembered someone giving him this advice. "Just roll with the punches, and you'll be OK, kid." He figured he had been at least that, OK.

He turned a bit to see the streetlights in the smoky distance through his open window. He slept off and on throughout the night. Between the colloquial rhythms, the mixture of smells, and the light coming in from the outside that kept his room dimly lit, it was no wonder why. It was either that or close the window and suffer the still, stagnant heat of the ninety-degree night. In his view, he simply chose the lesser of two evils, but the next night that could change.

He heard footsteps then turned his head slightly to the door to see his mother's hand, and then arm slide through the barely opened door and flip up the light switch. The brightness caused his eyes to shut immediately. He wasn't sure if it was the light or his anticipation of the light that caused him to close his eyes. A split second later he heard a calm, but authoritative, voice say,

"Wake up, baby."

He instinctively sat up, rubbed his closed eyes, and dreaded opening them. He only now appreciated his drifting and rolling. "I'm up, Ma," he replied and waited for the customary *"get up now"* from her, which usually followed. It was a verbal morning dance that had become commonplace, but the response never came.

Something was unusual this morning—a bit off. Maybe he was sick. Maybe it was the heat. Maybe he didn't get enough sleep. It was, the first day of school, but he had had first days of school before. But this was the first day at a new school. *Yes,* he thought, *that's it,* and he opened his eyes. *She doesn't wanna put too much pressure on me. How nice of Momma.*

He was amazed at the difference the light caused in his room compared to the light that had shone through the night. His mind wondered about all the different shades in the world between dark and light, black and white, and wrong and right. *Could it be like that with all things?* He had heard somewhere that the world was full of different shades of gray. But he had also heard the exact opposite— that there were no shades, only black and white, especially when it came to wrong and right. *It's all so confusing ... which makes it good to be a kid and not have to worry about those things.* "But I am worrying about it." He shook his head as if to come to his senses.

Eyes adjusted to the light, he jumped up from his bed since he didn't want to take advantage of his mother's kindness or incur her wrath. Just before he walked out of his bedroom, he noticed how empty and plain his room was and then he turned off his light. It wasn't always that way, but now there was nothing on his nightstand, save a Bible. There was nothing on his dresser. And with the exception of a certificate from the Department of Health Vital Records, there was nothing on his walls, no plaques, no posters, not even a picture or painting. But he knew it had to be that way because of his problem.

*That's what they call it ... a problem. It isn't a problem for me. I never hurt myself or anyone else when I was sleepwalking. I may have broken a few things, but they were my things.* "That's right, my things," he said, feeling a little irritable. *They were things that I earned, won, or traded up for at school or in the Exclave.* "My things," he said again and even louder this time as if to sound off to someone who might be listening. But there was no one.

There was a strange silence—an awkward silence that punctuated this strange Tuesday morning.

If he kept this up, he realized he would call into play another problem, so he tried to calm himself. He entered the bathroom and flipped on the light. Still, he couldn't stop thinking about his empty room with no chess set on his dresser, no dart game or calendar on his wall, no guitar leaning against his closet door, not even an alarm clock on his nightstand. *What teenager doesn't have a clock on their nightstand? Why would Momma do this? I guess it makes sense. She must have her reasons. Momma never does anything unless she figures she has a good reason. A good reason is more important to Momma than right or wrong.*

He stood in front of the sink, turned on the water, and looked into the mirror with a blank stare. He noticed that three hairs had begun to grow on his chin, and he smiled. He had never thought much of himself. He didn't see himself as special in any way. He saw himself as an average kid. He wasn't too dark or too light, but right in the middle, brown-skinned he liked to say. He was average height, average weight, average everything, and he liked it that way. He felt that if he didn't stand out, then he couldn't get into much trouble, and he would be left alone. That was fine with him.

He did like his hair, though, and he hated every time he had to get it cut. He vowed when he got old enough he would never get it cut again, and in his mind, that time had come. He was a teenager now, and the next time he was told he had to get a haircut, he would stand his ground.

It had been a while since his last haircut, and his hair had grown at least an inch long. He liked the way it felt in his fingers, and he twisted the tufts around them all day long—even when he wasn't thinking about it. For this reason, no matter how often he picked or combed his hair, it was always twisted and lumpy. In the Exclave when the other boys played at insults, his hair was often the target. But he didn't mind because he liked his hair.

In Sunday School, the story that stuck most in his mind was the one about Samson and Delilah. He thought no story was better. He liked to call himself Naz because he read in the Bible that Samson was a Nazarite, and part of being a Nazarite meant never cutting one's hair. This made him love his hair all the more and in his mind gave him a logical reason for not wanting it cut.

He figured when haircut time came again—and it was fast approaching—he would tell a lie. He was no good at lying, so he worked it out in his mind ahead of time. He would tell of an angel or some spirit that had come to him in a dream and forbidden him from ever cutting it again, or terrible things would happen—not just to him but his family. He shuddered to think how wrong such a lie must be. Lying was a part of living in the Exclave. *You have to lie to survive you know but not this kind of lying, not about angels and spirits.* He didn't care. That's how much he liked his hair.

He never admitted to anyone that what fascinated him, even more, was how much Samson loved Delilah, so much so it cost him his life. But he would never cut his hair—*not even for the likes ... or the love of a Delilah.*

Hating his given name, he sometimes told people he met that his name was Sam, as Naz didn't always seem quite appropriate, especially with the grown-ups and Market Merchants.

Now, standing in the mirror, he studied himself as he picked up his toothbrush with one hand and the tube of toothpaste with the other. As he fumbled with the toothpaste, he looked down.

There were more things on the bathroom sink than on his bedroom nightstand. He bristled.

"They were my things," he said, once more looking at the bathroom door. "My things!" Then he let it go at that.

He put some toothpaste on his toothbrush and began to brush his teeth. Yes, there was something different today. As he brushed his teeth and studied his reflection in the mirror staring back at him, he noticed, out of the corner of his eye, the tube of toothpaste he had put down was rising again in his reflection but this time on its own. What was even stranger was the toothpaste hovering in midair next to his face did not seem all that odd to him.

In the back of his mind he could hear his mother saying something, but between brushing his teeth, the water running, and the suspended toothpaste, her words stayed right there—in the back of his mind.

On the other side of his head, a bar of soap mimicked the toothpaste. He smiled and twisted his hair with his free hand. He decided to step back and take it all in, but there was no floor, or at least he wasn't standing on it anymore. He, along with the soap and toothpaste, was suspended in midair. And if things weren't interesting enough, a bottle of mouthwash floated by on its side, and in the mirror, a towel sailed just over his head.

**HE BECAME CONCERNED** when he heard a rumbling sound growing steadily in the distance, making his mother's words through the closed bathroom door indistinct. It finally dawned on him—*it's an earthquake*—and fear claimed him for the first time. *An earthquake? No, never in the Exclave … a tornado, which would explain that rumbling sound getting louder.* He had heard about tornados before but never experienced one. *Is this what it's like … slow motion and things floating all around you? Momma must've been trying to warn me, direct me to safety. Is it too late for me to take cover?*

He panicked, and his mind raced, but all about him was in slow motion. He quickly reached for the door, or so he thought, but it was as if his mind and body were separate, and when he looked at his hand, it seemed like minutes went by as it traveled to reach the doorknob. When his hand finally reached the doorknob, he turned it and kept on turning it round and round. It spun around as if broken. He pulled the knob, but the door wouldn't open. He tried a second time then a third. He pulled it with all his might, but the door still would not budge. It wasn't locked, but he figured—*somehow with all that was going on, it must've gotten jammed.*

He yelled, "*Ma ... Ma ... Ma!*" But he couldn't hear the sound of his own voice, even though the rumbling sound that now resembled that of a train didn't seem loud enough to drown it out. He continued to yell, "*Ma ... Ma ... Ma!*" and wondered if she had given up on him. *She wouldn't have left me here, would she? She wouldn't have left me here to ... to ... unless she had good reason ... a really good reason.*

After wrestling with the door for what seemed like an eternity, he let go of the doorknob. The floor came apart beneath him. Feeling gravity return and take him down with, and through the floor, he tried to grab the doorknob once more, but it was too late. As he plummeted below, he saw seven distinct shadowy figures. He closed his eyes and braced for impact. Like his mother's response earlier, it never came, and he knew as he sat up in his bed, it was all a dream—*a stupid dream.* He liked dreams, though. They were one of his favorite things, next to his hair.

# 03: MISS TRACEY

Naz was wide-awake now, and something was wrong. He had done something, and he could sense it as he heard footsteps approaching his bedroom.

"It's time to get up; you're already late," a woman said coldly.

It was a voice he hardly recognized. It was not his mother. His mother wasn't there. And this time he wasn't dreaming. He was sure of it.

"I'm up," he replied. *If I'm going to be late, it's not going to be my fault.* He wasn't even allowed to use his alarm clock anymore. A clock he had gotten as a gift was now on a shelf in his closet for fear it would be knocked off his nightstand and broken during an episode of sleepwalking.

"You got up again last night, and you made a mess in the bathroom," said the woman on the other side of the door.

*Uh-oh.*

"That therapy isn't doing you a bit of good," she continued. "You've only been here two months, and that makes the third time. Maybe we should put a lock on your door."

*A lock ... that would be kinda cool. Then I could have more privacy. Maybe I could start putting things back up in my room, and nobody would know.* "Teenagers should have a little privacy," Naz said under his breath, and then louder he offered, "I'm sorry, ma'am," in the most apologetic tone he could muster, trying to butter her up so she would seriously consider putting that lock on his door.

As if she didn't hear him, she added in a scolding tone, "And you better put everything back the way it was *before* you go to school."

He could tell by the words she used it wasn't that bad, but she was what they called in the Exclave, "Drama."

"Yes, ma'am," Naz assured her, and within seconds he was on his way down the hallway to the bathroom to assess the damage.

She called to him from her bedroom. "And how many times do I have to tell you to stop calling me ma'am? I don't have any kids. I'm still a young woman."

Tracey Billings was a single woman, barely in her twenties, who worked as an executive assistant. She had discovered she could make extra money by taking in foster kids. She liked to think she had gotten a deal by taking in two at a time but often wondered if she had bitten off more than she could chew.

Naz answered, "Yes, ma ... I mean, Miss Tracey," as he entered the bathroom. Again he thought, *"Drama."* "Nope, it isn't that bad," he continued as if to convince himself. And it wasn't. Still, he didn't like not being in control and having what everyone liked to call "a problem."

The tube of toothpaste and his toothbrush were in the sink— *where they probably fell in my dream.* What he didn't understand was the soap, towel, and mouthwash. He never touched them in his dream, so they shouldn't have been out of place, but they were. *Isn't that how it works?* It was another question for his therapist.

Miss Tracey was right about one thing. Going to see a therapist wasn't working. He had been going for two years now, and he still walked in his sleep. Even worse, he still heard the voices, something he decided to keep to himself.

When Naz finished in the bathroom, he tiptoed down to the small bedroom at the other end of the hallway so he would not attract Miss Tracey's attention again. He could see the light coming from under the door. He put his ear to the wood and listened then made a fist to knock. His little sister woke up every morning to the alarm on her phone, and he could hear the faint but unmistakable sounds of the classic Motown song: *"Love Child,"—every morning the same song ... her favorite song.* Before his knuckles could meet the wood door, Meridian emerged fully dressed from the bedroom. She had a knack for beating him to the punch.

## 04: MERI

**M**eridian Liberty Slaughter was a fiery little girl who always spoke her mind. She never made excuses for herself, and it was her greatest ambition (one of many) to have her own law firm. Meridian wanted to be first at everything. She had lived in the Exclave her whole life and believed it was her destiny to make a difference there—in a big way. Her sandy red hair and caramel skin tone coupled with her active imagination and relentless nature earned her the nickname "Firecracker" at a very young age. At the age of three, she was diagnosed with a mild congenital heart defect but refused to let anyone baby her, especially Naz.

"Good morning," she beamed as if she had won some great prize the night before. Her eyes wide and step lively, she sped past before he had a chance to shush her. When she got to the bathroom door, she turned to him and continued in a low whisper, "I'm not thinkin' about her." She then ducked into the bathroom before he could respond.

He smiled and shook his head as he walked back down the hallway. He liked dreams a lot and his hair even more, but when it came to Meridian, she meant everything to him. Anything else was a distant second. In his mind, he was all she had, and she was all he had. He swore that she was a spry old lady in a little girl's body, and the old folks said she was an old soul that had been here before.

She started school at an early age, and because of the grades she received, Naz's guess was, she would probably finish even earlier. She was only nine and already in the fifth grade. She wanted to be a lawyer, singer, tennis pro, and chess grandmaster, but not eventually when she grew up. She wanted it right now. Naz knew that he needed to get her out of the Exclave as soon as possible. But he also knew it wouldn't be easy. It was her home and all she had ever known. She was always saying that, even if she left the Exclave for college or something, she would come back one day to make a difference.

They had a good morning system. Meridian showered the night before and Naz in the morning. They both awoke at the same time. He would go into the bathroom while she got dressed, and then they would switch, simple yet effective. In less than thirty minutes they would be walking out the door. They wouldn't bother with breakfast. They would get free breakfast at school. The less time spent at Miss Tracey's, the better. She couldn't cook anyway.

As they opened the door to leave, Miss Tracey, as if on cue, recited, "Be careful, Meri, and ..." she hesitated, as if she had forgotten or as if she didn't really want to say his name.

Before she could finish, Meri chimed, "His name is—"

Miss Tracey cut her off. "I know what his name is, little Miss Know-It-All. That's why I don't *have* kids." Her voice became muffled as the door closed behind them.

"Why are you always messing with her? I don't wanna have to move again," said Naz.

"Trust me. She's never had it so easy. We take care of ourselves. The two of us are easy money for her. So I'm gonna make her work at least a little for it," Meri said, laughing.

"Look." Naz pointed to the three baby hairs on his chin.

"What?"

He moved his chin closer to her face and continued to point, but she turned away from him.

"What are you doing?" he asked.

"Can you take my magnifying glass out of my backpack?" She laughed.

"Whatever." He grabbed her backpack and spun her around until she faced him. He shook his head and laughed, too.

The rising sun exposed the partly cloudy sky, and unlike the hot, humid day before, there was a noticeable chill in the air. It was like that in the Exclave. The temperature could change drastically from day to day. As the pair walked onto the sidewalk, their breath rose in a light mist before them. He stopped her with a motion of his hand and surveyed the scene. His actions more instinctual than anything, and he didn't understand why. He had heard of all the bad things that went on in the Exclave, but he had never witnessed one incident during the more than three years he'd lived there.

Naz saw two boys. One was a little taller than he was, and the other a little shorter, but husky with a Mohawk haircut. The boys were clearly older than Naz, and they were walking from the direction in which he and Meri would have to go to reach her bus stop. He pulled out his phone to see what time it was. He estimated they had just enough time to reverse their steps and head in the other direction around the block to her bus stop to avoid crossing the path of the two older boys.

"Let's go this way," he said as he steered her around. A car was parked across the street. There were always cars parked on the streets, nice cars. The people in the Exclave didn't have a lot of money, but they did have nice cars. *How is that?* He had never seen this car before. A man with a hat was sitting inside and looking at them. The man quickly looked away as he if he didn't want to be seen.

Naz turned away, dismissing his fear as unfounded, just a symptom of his paranoia. He had always been this way, though, or so he thought. He could only remember as far back as three years ago. It had been that long since he came to live in the Exclave with Meri, their mother, and Meri's father. Everything before that was a blank. "Repressed Memories" were what his therapist liked to call them. The only thing Naz knew was that he had not always lived in the Exclave. *What could have happened before I came here that made me so paranoid?*

"Always so suspicious," Meri said, shaking her head as they started up the block.

"*Únete a nosotros,*" said the taller boy, loud enough for Naz and Meri to hear but to no one in particular it seemed.

"Why would you say that?" Naz asked Meri, as he purposely ignored the boys.

"Please, my bus stop is that way." Meri pointed behind her with her thumb over her shoulder but didn't turn around. "What did you see this time?" she asked, just now turning her head.

"Nothin'. Don't worry about it."

"Well, innocent until proven guilty."

"Better safe than sorry," he shot back.

Meri one-upped Naz with embarrassing regularity, but he didn't mind. He wasn't sure if he allowed the privilege, or she indeed possessed the power to accomplish the feat. Knowing he would inevitably lose the battle of one-liners as he always did, he asked suddenly.

"Meri, what do you think about dreams?"

"Dreams?" she responded curiously. "You mean regular dreams or deluxe, king-sized, wake-up-everybody-else-in-the-house dreams?"

"I mean dreams, Meri," he said, laughing. "Do you think they mean anything?"

"How would I know? I'm only nine years old."

"Oh, only nine years old, huh? Now watch this. The next time you wanna do something that you know you're too young to do, you're gonna say, 'I'm almost ten years old.'" It was his best Meri imitation.

"All right, true story. I got this. What was your dream about?"

He had to stop and think. It was less than an hour ago, but he was already starting to forget the dream. He was like that when it came to his dreams.

After a few seconds, she asked sarcastically, "Now am I supposed to be reading your mind, too?"

"No, I was trapped in the bathroom, and there was an earthquake. I was falling, and there were seven people ... watching ... I think." He remembered the part about their mother but conveniently left it out.

"And that's it?" She instinctively knew he had left something out.

"Isn't that enough? I mean, picture it. You're locked in the bathroom, an earthquake hits, and stuff is flying all over the place. You're falling, and there are seven ..."

"And?"

"And you wake up. That's it."

"Who locked you in the bathroom? Was it Miss Tracey? 'Cause I'll beat her down for ya, you know," she said jokingly, as she balled up her fists and punched at the air repeatedly.

"No, I don't remember that part," he said, laughing along.

"Who else was in the dream?"

"Just me ... and the seven shadow people."

"Shadow people? Um ... let me think." She stopped walking, put two fingers from each hand on her temples, and closed her eyes.

He stopped a few feet in front of her, looked back at her, and shook his head in amusement. She opened her eyes after a few seconds and continued walking.

"I've got it," she said. "I don't know about the seven shadow people, but something big is about to happen in your life. That's the earthquake. The stuff, as you called it, flying all over the place means you've lost control. And finally," she paused. "Now this is the most important part." She paused again but then waited to speak.

"I'm listening."

"Being locked in the bathroom and falling symbolize your inadequacy to deal with the situation."

He looked at her with his mouth wide open for a second and then asked in disbelief, "You serious?"

"Nope, but it sounded real good, didn't it?" she said, laughing. "What do you think, psychiatrist or lawyer? I could be, like, the first behavioral attorney."

"More like the first psycho-lawyer."

They both laughed.

"And who's inadequate? Inadequacy? You're supposed to be helping me. Inadequacy ... where'd you learn that word anyway?" he added almost under his breath.

"You sure Miss Tracey didn't lock you in the bathroom?"

They both continued to laugh.

They approached Meri's bus stop just as the bus was arriving.

"Seriously, I don't think it means anything, just random 'stuff,' as you like to say. We all have dreams, right?" she asked.

"I don't know. What do you dream about?"

"Wouldn't you like to know?"

As the other kids began to get on the school bus, Naz began to grill her. "Do you have your money?"

"Yes."

"Where'd you put it?"

"In my sock like you told me," she said in a sassy tone.

"Remember, nobody will ever think to look for it there. Where's your phone?"

"In my pocket," she said, patting her left back pocket.

"Is it on vibrate?"

"Always."

He reached into his pocket and pulled out his phone to see what time it was again. "Did you charge it last night?"

"Of course I did. Did you charge yours?" she asked indignantly. "Momma never asked all these questions," she continued, with a cold look on her face.

"Momma's not here," he snapped. "She's not here," he repeated calmly. He looked at his phone again and noticed it only had two out of four bars lit up, indicating he had forgotten to charge it the night before. "And don't worry about my phone," he said with a sheepish grin on his face.

"Uh-huh," she said suspiciously.

Just as she was stepping onto the bus, she looked back at him and said, "By the way, I did get up last night when I heard you in the bathroom, but as usual, you had gone back to bed by the time I got there."

Her words got lost in his thoughts. He was still stuck on her mentioning their mother. *Why would she do that?* Because she knew how to get in his head, and she was the only one that could because she knew he cared. She was good at mind games, a natural. He cared because he knew it bothered her to mention their mother, even though she didn't show it.

Two years earlier they lost their mother and Meri's father in what the authorities called a freak accident. Since that day, Meri had never shed a tear, or at least she never let Naz see it. She was tough like that, and Naz felt that someday soon because she hadn't cried, she would have to go to therapy, too.

Naz had refused to call Meri's father anything other than Bearn. Most of the time he referred to Bearn as "him" or "he." Seeing him as a father figure just didn't feel right. But he never liked him either—with good reason—even before the accident. But he kept all that to himself. After all, he had been Meri's father. Naz had no memory of his own father.

The bus pulled away. *I have got to get her out of here.* He turned and walked in the other direction toward Lincoln Middle School.

*If she thinks she's going to Lincoln next year, she's mistaken.* Since she had started school, she never got less than an "A." His therapist was in the process of setting Meri up to take a test for International Academy, a private school outside of the Exclave. If she did well enough on the test and in an interview, she could receive a scholarship to attend school there the following year. Naz was determined that was the way it was going to be.

## 05: HAM

The Exclave was a sprawling, massive area covering over one hundred forty-four square miles with a population of more than a million people. Divided into nine boroughs and comprised of forty-two sections, it was a mosaic of different races, cultural groups, and factions—all fiercely territorial as evidenced by gang wars and incessant violence. In the midst of the differences and the chaos, the inhabitants shared one thing only. They were all poor, except for a fortunate few—and those who dealt in drugs.

Since coming to the Exclave three years ago, they were now in the fourth section in which they'd lived, and Naz was hoping it would be the last, if only for Meri's sake. As he walked, he worried about her first day at Higginbotham. *She'll be OK. How dangerous can elementary school be? I have to get her out of here.*

There was no doubt in his mind that she would pass the test and ace the interview for International Academy. He figured if they could continue staying at Miss Tracey's, he could find a way for her to get to and from International Academy every day for the next school year. He just knew it.

Meri always wanted to go where she thought Naz was going to be, and that was fine by him. The problem was he would go on to high school next year, Union High School to be exact. But what she wanted didn't matter to him. *If she thinks she's going to Lincoln Middle School next year, she has another thought coming.*

It was only eight blocks to Lincoln from Meri's bus stop. Naz had come to know this section well in the past two months. He saw the customary bums, panhandlers, homeless people, and broken men shuffling through the streets. He was always taught not to judge, but whenever he saw them, he couldn't help but think—*one day I'm going to help them somehow.* Then he wondered why no one else ever did. He would help them now if he could, but he didn't know how. *Maybe no one knows how, and that's why they're still here. Why can't they help themselves? And why are so few of them women? What do the women do when they're down and out ... kill themselves?* He handed one of the derelicts in the street all the loose change in his pocket. Then he laughed to himself as a provocatively dressed woman smiled and winked at him from across the street.

He passed by his house on his way back down the street. The strange car with the mysterious man in the hat was no longer there.

He walked one more block, turned right at the corner, and immediately saw Hector. Naz had a knack for seeing things before anyone else did. Hector Antonio Martinez, who had yet to notice Naz, was the first and only real friend Naz had made since he moved to Section 31. Hector was on his way to meet Naz so they could walk to Lincoln together. He called himself Ham because H.A.M. were his initials. However, everyone else called him that because he was a ham, an overly flamboyant kid who never seemed to run out of energy or things to say.

A nickname was important in the Exclave, but not just any nickname, it had to be the right nickname. The best and most respected nicknames were the ones given to you by someone else, someone who was also respected in the community. It might be a high school basketball star, a really cool teacher, or possibly even a drug dealer. The problem was they usually came up with something that seemed silly, like Cinnamon Roll or Water Bug—a name that Naz felt you had to wait out until it developed a ring to it. Naz didn't think there was anything special about the nickname he had given himself, only that it was special to him, and he hated his given name.

"¿Qué pasa, Naz?" Hector said as they approached each other. They simultaneously put their arms out to shake hands, Naz with his hand closed in a fist and Hector with his open.

"What's up, Ham?" Naz replied awkwardly in response to the botched handshake.

"Habla español mi amigo."

"Look, we either get the Spanish right or the handshake," Naz replied with a smile.

Ham prided himself on his culture and had been trying to teach Naz Spanish since the first day they met.

"Here, let me show you," said Ham. "You don't wanna blow this on your first day of school. Rep is all a Railsplitter has," he continued, as he demonstrated the latest handshake.

"A Rail what?" asked Naz, his attention split between the crash course on handshake etiquette and whatever else Ham was talking about.

Like Meri, Ham was born in the Exclave and knew nothing else. His parents migrated from Mexico while his mother was pregnant with him. There were seven younger brothers and sisters, and his proud family was of Mayan descent, a fact Ham mentioned daily as a reminder of this. His family spoke fluent Spanish, something common among the Hispanic population of the Exclave.

"A Railsplitter, and as of today, you are an official Lincoln Railsplitter," proclaimed Ham.

In a lot of ways Ham reminded Naz of Meri. They both possessed a surplus of energy and no matter what was going on, both found a way to see something positive in it.

"You excited?" Ham prodded. After a short pause, he continued, "Of course you are. Who wouldn't be? This is the first day of school. We talkin' *chicas calientes, chicas calientes, y más chicas calientes* ... not like those *pollos* at Trenton."

Ham often broke into Spanish without warning. Not knowing Spanish well at all, Naz more often than not had to use context clues to translate, and he had gotten pretty good at it. This time he was pretty sure Ham was talking about girls.

Naz had attended Monticello the first half of his seventh-grade year and transferred to Trenton Middle School for the second half of that year. He nodded in agreement with Ham. There hadn't been much to look at the year before in the way of pretty girls.

Naz didn't say much, partly because Ham never stopped talking, and partly because that's just the way he was—unless he was with Meri. He would talk to Meri. With others, he often answered questions in his mind without saying the words, which made people think he wasn't paying attention, was ignoring them, or was just being plain rude. It was another habit he couldn't remember picking up or where, for that matter.

"What about basketball? You tryin' out?" Ham asked. "We had the squad last year, only lost one game, and if I would've been on the team, we would've won 'em all. We blew Trenton out *and* won the fight after the game. They weak! I'm gonna get my grades this year, though."

Ham often had a way of stretching the truth, but he was dead on when it came to basketball. He was good, very good. He had spent most of his time playing basketball at the park during the summer, that is, when he wasn't harassing the *chicas,* as he called them. He always got chosen first for pickup games, and he carried a basketball around wherever he went. In fact, this was the first time Naz could remember ever seeing Ham without a ball. Even more amazing was Ham's height—almost a head shorter than Naz—something Ham attributed to his Mayan heritage. But his lack of stature didn't stop him on the court.

"What do you mean?" Naz asked.

"My grades, they were bad ... I guess. So they wouldn't let me play. Besides, the teachers didn't like me either. But this year I got it all figured out. I'm gonna hook up with the smartest *chica* until we get our first report card. The smartest *chicas* are the easiest to get 'cause they're the ugliest, right? Then, after I get my grades, I can dump her. I'm a genius," he said, laughing.

Naz could not relate to what Ham had just said. *Genius? If he wanted better grades, why didn't he just study harder?* Then it occurred to him that Ham was fourteen, more than a year older than Naz, but in the same grade. Somewhere along the way Ham had been kept back. Naz wondered if grades were the reason: it seemed to make sense. Between the excuses and bad grades in school, Ham was starting to seem less and less like Meri.

"So?" Ham prodded.

"So what?"

"You gonna try out?"

Naz thought he had answered the question but obviously only in his mind again. "I don't think so."

"Can you even play?"

"I don't know. I've never tried."

"Then you can't. It ain't like riding a bike or hanging out at the market. You have to practice ... a lot if you wanna be good like me. I've been playin' ball all my life ... gonna make it to the league one day."

Confidence was one thing Ham wasn't short on.

Naz was more than intrigued when he first saw Ham play at the park, but between running errands for the Market Merchants to earn money and hanging out with Meri, there just wasn't enough time for basketball. He was starting to tune out on Ham's words. It was something he often did if Ham talked too long. Naz decided to change the subject.

"What do you think about dreams?" Naz asked.

Ham didn't know about Naz's voices or his sleepwalking. Only the therapists, Meri, Miss Tracey, and his last two foster families were aware of his "problems." Naz knew that you just didn't go around telling your friends about things like that. But when it came to dreams, he thought it was a safe topic to discuss—*everybody dreams.* He knew Ham would have something to say on the subject, just as he did about everything else.

"What about 'em?" asked Ham.

"Do you have 'em?"

"Everybody has 'em. Some people never remember their dreams, and others remember them as clearly as if they really happened."

"Do you think they mean anything?"

"Naw, they're just a bunch of pictures, ideas ... thoughts and emotions ... I think. They're stored up somewhere between your conscious and subconscious mind and become randomly active when you sleep. Then your brain acts like an iPod shuffle and plays whatever pops up next ... or something like that."

Ham was no dummy. He knew a lot about a lot of things, and this made Naz wonder about Ham's grades all the more.

Baiting him, Naz said, "Tell me about one of your dreams."

"I don't ever remember my dreams. Do you?"

*Perfect.* "One dream." He looked up and nodded his head. Almost drawing a complete blank, he could barely remember the dream he just had the night before, the dream he had just told Meri about. "Somebody locked me in my bedroom, and then seven people broke in the house ... I think, and I couldn't get out to help." He paused. "Oh, and there's stuff flying around."

"What do you mean, stuff? What kinda stuff?"

Naz honestly had no idea now. He just remembered telling Meri about stuff flying around.

"Just stuff," Naz answered and then added, "Never mind about the stuff."

"OK, let me get this right. Somebody locked you in your bedroom while seven people were breaking in your house ... and there's no stuff, right?"

"Right."

"Who locked you in your bedroom? Miss Tracey?" Ham laughed.

"No. I'm not sure." Naz laughed. "I don't remember."

"Well, how did you know it was seven people if you were locked in the bedroom?"

Naz paused and tugged at his hair. "I can't remember that either." He laughed again.

"Hmmm ... as my dad would say, it looks to me like you're up a creek without a paddle."

"What does that mean?"

"That means you got a problem with no solution, *amigo.*" Ham laughed again. "But like I said, dreams don't mean nothin'."

# 06: GANG

As they walked up the street, Naz saw the two boys he had avoided earlier walking toward them.

Ham continued, "I read—"

Naz cut in jokingly. "You read, Ham?"

Ham gave a phony laugh and then continued, "That's funny, Sam-I-Don't-Remember-Who-I-Am. Like I was saying, I read somewhere that sometimes people actually know when they're dreaming and can control parts of the dream."

Naz watched the two boys as they continued to approach. They were a block away. *Why would they be here in this section ... today ... so early in the morning? If they're new to this section and on their way to Union High School—a half mile away—they should have been long gone by now.* He had seen them only twenty minutes ago two blocks away. *Why are they still here? Something's wrong. It doesn't feel right.*

Ham continued. "I think they call it—"

"Let's cross here." Naz began to nudge Ham.

Ham nudged back. "Like I was saying, I think they call it lucid dreaming."

"Enough about dreams. Let's cross here."

"Why? Lincoln's on this side."

"I know, but ..." He didn't know what else to say to persuade Ham to cross the street. But something was wrong. He could somehow sense the emergence of danger. He could feel it, and he knew now he wasn't going to be able to get Ham to cross. Ham was no coward. Naz had never seen it for himself but had heard from others in Section 31 that Ham was good in a fight and had the scars, including a nasty one under his right eye, to prove that he had been in wars. Naz had never been in a fight, at least not one that he could remember.

Ham noticed the two boys in front of them and caught on, only he had a different reaction. "Cross for them? This is our section. We ain't goin' nowhere." Ham's whole attitude and body language changed, and instead of slowing, he sped up a bit. It was another side of him that Naz had only heard about but had never seen.

"What are you gonna do?" Naz asked nervously.

"Nothin'. We're just on our way to school talking about dreams is all, right?"

The boys were now within a half block of each other.

"Have you ever had a lucid dream?" Ham asked, as he slowly reached into his back pocket.

"A what?" Naz asked in confusion.

Ham continued the conversation as if nothing had changed. "A lucid dream, you know, when you actually know you're dreaming."

Out of the corner of his eye, Naz saw Ham pull a black object out of his back pocket and hold it behind his back. Naz and Ham were now about fifty feet from the two boys. They were even bigger and possibly older than Naz first thought, but that didn't seem to bother Ham.

"I don't ... I ... I don't think I ever had that dream ... before." Naz struggled to speak not even knowing what he was saying.

When the boys were within thirty feet of each other, Ham said something in Spanish, something that came out very fast that Naz didn't understand. His hope that it was a peaceful greeting faded when he saw the reflection off a shining blade—a blade from the black object Ham was concealing behind his back. The husky boy in front of Ham said something back in Spanish—something Naz remembered the taller boy saying earlier.

"*Únete a nosotros,*" said the husky boy.

Then, as if on cue, like something out of a Western, they all stopped about fifteen feet from each other. The two strange boys and Ham were smiling at one another, and Naz hoped that it was because they knew each other. But he was soon certain that wasn't the case, especially when the taller boy, who was also concealing something behind his back, began to taunt Naz and started moving slowly from facing him to Naz's side. His voice was unusually gruff, as he was laughing and speaking in Spanish. Naz was confused. *Is this a robbery?* He didn't have a whole lot of money. He didn't understand what this was all about.

Naz said, "*No hablo español.*"

It was something he remembered Ham teaching him, but the boy just continued to laugh. The taller boy was apparently trying to angle around and get behind Naz, but with the boy's every move, Naz turned to face him.

Suddenly Ham and the husky boy with the Mohawk pulled their knives and crouched in some sort of attack position. They were still smiling and still making verbal exchanges in Spanish.

That's when it happened. Naz hadn't heard the voices in almost two months, and now they were back. It always seemed to happen when he was scared or angry, but there were other times, too.

"*He's mad,*" the voice said.

Naz was angry because he allowed himself to get involved in something like this. He had avoided similar confrontations for over three years, and now he was smack dab in the middle of one.

"*He's scared,*" the voice said.

Naz was scared because he didn't know what would happen to Meri if something happened to him. That was unthinkable, and he became even angrier, his fingernails digging into his palms. He needed to find a way out of this. His mind raced, but everything around him was in slow motion, just like his dream from the night before. He now recalled it vividly. But he wasn't dreaming, and he knew it.

*"He doesn't understand us,"* the voice continued.

*Are there voices ... or just one voice?* He wished he had taken Ham's efforts to teach him Spanish more seriously, and he vowed to do just that if he ever ... *no, when I get out of this. If I could just speak Spanish, I know I could talk my way out of this.*

*"You can't fight,"* said the voice.

He needed to find another way.

*"You better not run,"* the voice said.

*That's a good idea. I can run.* He was fast, real fast. He had always been faster than anybody in his class. But he couldn't leave Ham, even though it was Ham who had gotten him into this mess. Still, he needed to find a way out, another way.

*"You're going to die,"* said the voice.

All of a sudden, the husky boy lunged at Ham with his knife. Barely moving, Ham slid to the side evading the husky boy's attack and ended up right next to the boy.

Between the voices and the commotion of the fight, Naz lost sight of the taller boy. He had suddenly grabbed Naz from behind and was holding the point of his knife at Naz's throat while jabbing and just breaking the skin.

*"Don't move, or you're going to die,"* said the voice.

*"¡ÚNETE A NOSOTROS!"* yelled the taller boy as he continued to hold Naz.

Meanwhile, Ham elbowed the husky boy in the nose, causing him to drop his knife and fall to his knees. The boy writhed on the ground, covering his face with his hands.

*"Oh, my God,"* the voice continued.

As the boy holding Naz tightened his grip, Naz could feel the searing sting from the tip of the knife. He wasn't sure if it was blood, sweat, or a combination of the two running down his neck. He tried to block out the voices, but now there were more of them, and they were growing even louder.

Ham yelled something in Spanish to the boy that was holding Naz. Naz could only assume he'd said to let him go.

*"What should I do now?"* the voice yelled and then, *"Blood!"*

Naz tried to see if the voices were coming from one of the boys. They weren't. They were all speaking in Spanish, and he didn't understand any of it.

*"Blood!"* the voice screamed again. The voices were in his head, and they were distracting him.

The boy yelled something back at Ham. Ham repeated himself, and it turned into a shouting match.

*"But he's too little,"* the voice said.

By this time the boy on the ground had made it to his knees. He was holding his bloodied nose and creeping toward his knife. The knife was lying on the ground several feet away.

"Ham!" Naz yelled, but it was too late.

*"He's a coward,"* said the voice.

With one quick move, the boy picked up his knife and stabbed Ham just above his belt.

*"Oh, my God!"* said the voice.

Ham let out a terrible scream. "AAAAAAAAARGH!" He fell on his side and curled into a fetal position.

All of a sudden the husky boy that had stabbed Ham took off running down the street yelling, *"¡Roffio, vamos! ¡Roffio, vamos!"*

Without warning, the boy who held Naz threw him to the ground and ran down the street after the other boy.

At first, Naz didn't move. Then, he felt the sharp sting on his neck and instinctively brought his hand up to touch the puncture wound that was now oozing blood. He tentatively looked down and saw the trail of blood that stained his gray shirt a dark, maroon hue. *Am I OK? Is this what shock feels like?* He had never seen anything like this, much less been in the middle of it.

*"Look ... blood,"* the voice said.

Naz heard Ham moan. He tried to shake the voices out of his head as he stood up and stumbled over to Ham who was writhing in pain.

"Look ... blood ... he's bleeding," Naz heard a girl say.

Kids gathered around. Some walked by and pointed, probably on their way to school.

"*Blood,*" the voice muttered.

He didn't know what to do. *It's not like the movies now.* There was no hero, no music, no riding away. There was just blood, every-where, his blood, the husky boy's blood, and Ham's blood, a lot of Ham's blood. It was thick and dark red.

"*Blood,*" Naz heard the voice say again.

"Somebody call an ambulance!" a lady in the distance screamed. He didn't know what to say to Ham who was clearly not OK.

"*I'm scared,*" the voice whispered.

He kneeled down with his hand still on his neck. With his free hand, he grabbed Ham's hand. It was cold. He didn't know what to do after that. Ham was still moving, and that made him feel a little better.

"Ham," Naz called.

Ham moaned.

"*I'm scared,*" said the voice again.

"Ham," Naz called again, and again Ham moaned. Ham had wet his pants. Between that, the blood, the sweat, and the smell, it made Naz feel sick, nauseous. He turned to the side and threw up. But he wouldn't leave Ham's side.

"*I'm scared,*" the voice said one more time.

With his mouth dry and soured with the taste of vomit, Naz yelled, "Somebody call an ambulance," and then louder, "Somebody call an ambulance!" and then as loud as he could, "SOMEBODY CALL AN AMBULANCE!"

"*Somebody call an ambulance,*" the voice murmured. Then it was gone, and there was silence. Looking to his side, Naz saw a man drive by on the street. It was the same man that had been parked in front of his house earlier—*what does únete a nosotros mean?*

## 07: FEARS

M r. Andersen," the voice bellowed, snapping Naz back to reality. "For the third time, that is your name, isn't it, Son?"

When Naz looked up, the entire class was staring at him. He had apparently been daydreaming about what had happened earlier that morning and missed something. He saw the towering figure clad in a royal blue T-shirt and royal blue fleece pants in front of the classroom. The figure's eyes fixed on Naz. Naz decided to take a chance.

"I'm sorry, Sir. I don't know the answer."

Students began to snicker and mutter to each other as the tall man walked to the middle of the classroom where Naz was sitting. He needed only to wave his hand, and the noise from the students subsided immediately. With Naz looking up at him, the man could now see the blood seeping through the bandage on Naz's neck. Naz lowered his head in an attempt to conceal the bandaged wound.

"You are correct, Mr. Andersen. You are sorry. But why are you sorry?" The teacher spoke in a calm, low tone that almost seemed friendly. But Naz knew that wasn't the case, so he tried to steel himself for what was about to come.

"Um ... for not knowing the answer, Sir," Naz said.

"The answer to what, Son?"

Naz was caught. He had no idea what the question was, let alone the answer, so he decided to shake his head and hope he would be let off the hook. A long silence followed, so Naz thought he'd better at least say something. "I wasn't paying attention, Sir."

"Obviously, but the question at hand was not a question at all, Mr. Andersen but a directive ... a directive for you to tell us one interesting thing you did this summer."

*I should have known it was something like that. It is the first day of school.*

"So, enlighten us, Mr. Andersen."

Naz was stumped. A whole summer had gone by, and he couldn't think of one interesting thing he had done. He shook his head and replied, "Nothing."

"Come on now, Mr. Andersen, there must have been something. Did you travel somewhere, visit a relative ... go to an amusement park?" the teacher asked as he walked toward the back of the room and waited for a reply.

"I went to see my uncle in Washington D.C. ..." Naz said quickly, and then to make it more convincing and believable, he added, "... with my little sister." He felt like everyone in the classroom knew that he was lying, and it made him hot all over.

"And what did you see in D.C.?"

"Um ... um ... um ... The White House ... a monument ... and ..." He saw a picture of Abraham Lincoln on the wall, and in a flash, it came to him from nowhere. "The Lincoln Memorial, the Tomb of the Unknown Soldier, the Pentagon, the—"

"Thank you ... Mr. Andersen! I will say this one more time for the benefit of Mr. Andersen and anyone else who was out to lunch the first time." He pointed to the name printed on the dry-erase board in large capital letters.

# FEARS

Marcus Fears was the most respected and feared teacher at Lincoln. He was also the boys' basketball coach. To him, basketball was a microcosm of life, and he never missed an opportunity to take advantage of a teaching moment—on or off the court.

"I like to give my students choices ... my choices. You can address me in one of three ways: Mr. Fears, Coach Fears, or Coach, and that is all. Sir, was my father's name," said Fears as he looked at Naz.

Naz wondered how he had missed all of that. He had been there for the whole second half of the day, but it was as if he hadn't been there at all. His mind was still out on that street—in the Exclave, the battlefield. He kept rewinding it in his mind and playing it back, over and over again. His mind would retell how the ambulance came almost an hour after being called, with the police close behind. *Ham could've died. And they asked so many questions.* It was only the second time he had ever talked to a police officer, and as before, their presence alone made him feel like he was the one in trouble. They kept saying that they would catch the boys who did this, but it was well known in the Exclave that the police never caught anyone.

Fears' bellowing voice cut through again, startling Naz back to reality once more. "This is your last hour class of the day, Health 101, and I am here to teach you all one important thing this year, Railsplitters." He seemed to take pride in referring to the students as Railsplitters.

This took Naz's mind back to Ham who had first said the name to him earlier that morning.

"Risk Reduction," Fears continued. "Mr. Andersen, what one important thing will you learn this year?"

*He must've seen me daydreaming again.* "Uh ... Risk Reduction?"

"Are you asking me or telling me, Mr. Andersen?"

"Uh ... telling you, Sir ... I mean, Mr. ..." Naz looked at the board and quickly added, "Fears."

"Right! Risk Reduction, and how so?" He turned to the rest of the class. "Anyone have a clue?" He looked around as he continued to pace back toward the middle of the room.

None of the students raised their hands. Naz couldn't remember Fears sitting down since the class began—*almost a half hour ago.*

"No, you wouldn't ... mainly because I haven't told you yet," Fears continued. He spoke in barely more than a whisper at times, but no one seemed to have any trouble hearing him.

Between the pauses of his carefully chosen words, you could hear a pin drop. There was no movement whatsoever in the classroom other than Fears quietly pacing through the maze of desks and the heads of the students as they turned in sync to follow his every move. It was as if time were frozen. The students seemed transported to a static hypnotic dimension with Fears the only navigator.

"I can tell you to wear a bicycle helmet to save you from splitting your skull in half when you land on the cement after your bike hits a rock or pothole," Fears lectured and pointed out the window, as some of the students winced and grimaced in imaginary pain. "But you won't. Helmets look silly anyway."

Some students laughed nervously. He stopped his pacing to look at one student's hands in a loathsome manner then continued. "To prevent you from catching a cold, I can tell you to wash your filthy hands when you wake up in the morning. I can tell you to wash them before and after you eat. I can tell you to wash them after you use the bathroom and again before you go to bed at night." He turned to a girl who had just finished blowing her nose. "But you will not."

One student sat in the front row and never looked up while Fears was talking. Naz couldn't quite see the boy's face, but his hair was extremely short on the sides much like a soldier's but longer and all spiky on top like porcupine needles. Naz twisted a tendril of his own hair. It looked like the boy was writing in a notebook—*maybe taking notes*. But it didn't look like he was paying attention.

Naz saw him in class last hour, sitting in the front row doing the exact same thing. But no one, including Fears, found his behavior odd, unacceptable, or even interesting, except Naz. It was as if he was invisible, in his own world. Naz realized, if he continued to focus on the boy in the front row, he would hear it from Fears real soon again, so he turned his attention back to Fears.

Fears, now standing in the middle of the room, turned around and walked slowly backwards. When he reached a large, round boy with dark, curly hair, he stopped. It was as if Fears had eyes in the back of his head. He wheeled around and put out his hand. The boy looked up, and realizing he had been discovered, he pulled a half-eaten candy bar from underneath his desk and put it in Fears' hand.

"I can try to convince you to eat right and exercise," Fears continued as he looked at the boy. "But most of you will not." His voice was slowly getting louder with each phrase as if he were a preacher in church and about to reach a crescendo. "I can ask you ... no, implore that you say 'no' to drugs, but some of you will inevitably say 'yes.' And for my guys ... and girls, the gangs of the Exclave are *not* your family. Your family is at home where you live, and here with your classmates and teachers. Gangs are to be avoided at all cost. They are for the weak-minded follower, and here at Lincoln *we* are *all* leaders." He had a flair for the dramatic that captivated his students.

Fears' last words caught Naz's attention and sent him elsewhere again. *Gang?*

"But let me make this perfectly clear," Fears continued. "While you are here at Lincoln, you will respect the rules of this classroom and this school. You will respect yourselves and everyone else for that matter. And when I say Risk Reduction, it will do you good to know that your very life depends on it, Mr. Andersen!" Fears bellowed. "Is there a problem?"

Naz, snapping back to reality once more, realized he had just been staring out the window and replaying the morning's events in his brain again. On this first day of class he had been caught breaking Fears' biggest rule about not paying attention not once, but twice.

"No, Sir, I mean, Mr. Fears." Naz reached up to feel the blood now leaking from under his bandage.

The girl next to him saw it and turned away as if she didn't want Naz to notice she saw it.

"May I be excused, Sir?" asked Naz.

"By all means ... *sir*," Fears replied in a sarcastic, yet conciliatory tone. The students muttered to each other, as Fears was silent while Naz hurried out of the classroom into the half-deserted hallways of Lincoln.

# 08: LINCOLN

He looked in the mirror in the dimly lit bathroom and thought everything seemed washed out—not as vibrant or colorful as before, even his own appearance. *Is it my imagination?* It didn't help that he always wore dark or drab colors, his ongoing attempt at anonymity. *I've changed somehow. How could I have gone through that and not have changed?*

He removed the bandage and changed the dressing with the ointment and new bandage the paramedic had given him. The man told him the wound wasn't that bad and would heal in a week or so if he kept it clean and dressed.

After the fight that morning, Naz had snuck back home to change his bloodied shirt. While climbing out of his bedroom window, he'd half torn off the first bandage. Miss Tracey didn't trust him with a key yet, and he wasn't sure if she ever would. He waited until he knew she was gone before he went back. He didn't want any trouble, and a knife wound on his neck, serious or not, along with a bloodied shirt would certainly spell trouble. He made sure he didn't leave any signs that indicated he had come back home. On the way back to school he tossed the bloodied, Henley T-shirt into the first dumpster he came across. He would replace it later with money he earned from the Market Merchants.

As he stared in the mirror—*únete a nosotros. What could that mean?* Then he went back even further in his mind to the minutes before the stabbing occurred. What could he have done differently to prevent what had happened, to get Ham to cross that street, and to keep him from confronting those boys? *How is Ham?* He would call him later, then again, maybe not. Would Ham be angry with him for not fighting back? Would he blame Naz for everything? *But what could I have done? I didn't have a knife. Maybe I should carry a knife from now on.* "No, no, no. I've never even held a knife like that." *I would've gotten stabbed for sure, or even worse, and Meri would be alone now.*

No matter how he turned things over in his mind, he still felt responsible for Ham. *It took me too long to call Ham's mom.* She arrived frantic, just before the ambulance. "I just couldn't think. Maybe Ham can teach me how to use a knife when he gets ..." he paused. *The paramedic did say he'd be OK.*

Still, Naz couldn't help feeling like he was a coward because he wanted to cross the street to avoid the whole situation while Ham was willing to stand and fight. He felt like a coward because he had thought about running and because he had been so scared.

Finally, he stood straight up and stared confidently at himself. "That's dumb," he said aloud to his reflection. "That's stupid. I'm never carrying a knife. If there is a next time, coward or not, I'm going the other way, and whoever's with me can go their way. That's what I'll do." When he made up his mind to do something, he usually did it.

Naz realized he had been standing at the mirror a while and that he had better get back before class was over. He was already on the bad side of what seemed to be the most respected, and even worse, most feared teacher in the school. He didn't want to push his luck.

But there was something about Fears that wasn't so bad. There was something about him that was almost familiar, something he couldn't quite pinpoint.

He walked out of the bathroom and felt renewed. He had just about survived his first day of school at Lincoln, even though it had only been a half-day for him. As he walked down the hallway, he began to feel like himself again, finally able to take in the scene around him.

The hallways seemed less deserted to him than before he went into the bathroom. A security guard sat at a desk, but she was oblivious to the students that walked by randomly or stood in plain sight at their lockers. *She obviously doesn't want any trouble.* He caught the eye of a boy who was flirting with a girl in a stairwell, and he immediately looked the other way, not wanting any trouble himself. At a group of lockers directly across from the stairwell, a girl smoked a cigarette. Another girl played with her phone, and a boy with headphones, apparently listening to music, bobbed his head in a consistent rhythm.

Like the houses in the Exclave, all of the middle schools were identical. The long, ancient hallways of Lincoln, along with the lockers, lights, and doors that lined them, were a carbon copy of Trenton and Monticello, the last two schools that he had attended. The only difference was the school's color scheme. There were also pictures, paintings, and plaques all over the walls, past and present heroes of the school. He looked at the floor under his feet and made out a large caricature of a pale, bearded man with a big head and an even larger ax in his hands. *Abraham Lincoln, the Railsplitter.* It was funny-looking. It made him smile for the first time since this morning's incident, and he knew everything would be OK. That's when he looked up and saw—

# 09: AN ANGEL

Naz saw her at the drinking fountain. She had thick, bushy, dark hair that was pulled back and gathered into a long ponytail. The nerdy glasses she wore did a poor job of disguising how beautiful she really was. He felt like he was going to suffocate, but it was a good feeling, one he had never experienced before. Just as in his dream and the Exclave earlier that morning, things slowed down. And they were back, the voices. He'd never heard them twice in one day before, but the voices were the last thing on his mind right now.

"*What are you looking at?*" said the voice.

The water from the drinking fountain bubbled up, hit her barely parted lips and then cascaded back down. Then, unexpectedly, the water shot out of the fountain and hit her in the face. Composed, she stood up and looked at the fountain curiously. With her hand, she wrung the dripping water from her face. She turned and looked at Naz.

"*What are you looking at?*" the voice said again.

His eyes were glued to her as he inhaled deeply but did not exhale. He thought his furiously pounding heart would stop, and he felt an unfamiliar stirring in his middle. Without hesitation, she walked toward him. He was a deer, petrified in the headlights of a speeding car.

*"Well, don't just stand there; say something,"* the voice said.

She walked right up to him, took his hand, and said, "Come with me."

*"Can you talk?"* the voice asked.

He was in a trance, and in an instant, he finally understood what Samson must have felt for Delilah.

She led him down the hallway at a hurried pace, all the while holding his hand until they reached a door. It was there she stopped him by putting her hand on his chest. "I have to pee, and I don't want anyone to come in. Wait for me and knock on the door if someone comes," she said, as she walked through the door of the girls' bathroom.

Naz finally exhaled. He didn't hear the voices anymore, but his thoughts were in overdrive. *What just happened? This has to be a dream.* But Naz always knew when he wasn't dreaming; he just wasn't always sure when he was, so he reasoned to himself he was definitely not dreaming. *What if somebody came by and saw me just standing here, waiting next to the girls' bathroom? What would they think?* He was already on Fears' bad side, and now he had been gone for what seemed like a long time. But he didn't care. He wasn't moving until she came back out of the bathroom. That was his only assignment right now, and he was determined to do it well. Then, just as quickly as it all started, it ended.

"Thank you," she said, as she rushed out of the bathroom, ran past him down the hallway, and disappeared around another corridor.

Naz was stunned, frozen. The school bell rang startling him. Naz knew he and Fears were going to have a conversation—most likely a one-way conversation.

All summer long Naz heard stories of how Lincoln was one of the most popular middle schools in the Exclave, but he had no idea why. Every seat was filled in each of his classes, and now with-in a matter of seconds, the hallways were jam-packed with people. There were students, as well as teachers, going in both directions. Students lingered at their lockers. There were students still flowing out of classrooms. There seemed to be waves of students as far as the eye could see. *It was never like this at Trenton or Monticello.* He had also heard that students often lied about where they lived so they could go to Lincoln.

But in the midst of the bustling students and teachers, head and shoulders above them all, Fears emerged. He hugged some students and shook the hands of others. He even greeted fellow teachers as he slowly made his way down the packed hallway. Not only did he stand out in stature, but he had a voice that stood out as well. His thunder-ous voice carried above all the rest of the end-of-the-day noise and commotion. It was clear the same sovereignty and respect he com-manded in the classroom reigned supreme over the hallways of Lin-coln as well. Moses parting the Red Sea came to Naz's mind, as Fears moved ahead unfettered. Naz wondered if Fears had anything to do with the legendary fame of Lincoln Middle School.

Naz came up with an idea. He would walk by Fears slouched down and with his head turned the other way until he got back to the classroom. With any luck the door would still be open, he could make off with his books and then exit at the opposite end of the building. The chances were good the next day Fears would never re-member Naz hadn't come back before the bell rang. Naz hoped. He passed Fears, and the plan seemed to be going well—that is until he heard the thunder.

"Andersen!" bellowed Fears. "You left your books in my room."

Naz stopped dead in his tracks, stood erect, and turned to look at Fears. Fears continued to wade through the students going in the opposite direction as if he'd never turned to see Naz. With that, Naz continued down the hallway shaking his head with a sheepish grin on his face. He entered Fears' empty classroom, went to his desk and picked up the two textbooks and notebook he had been given earlier that day.

Naz turned to leave. A composition notebook still occupied the desk of the boy with the spiky military haircut. He turned and glanced through the open door into the bustling hallway and then looked back at the notebook once more. He figured he had enough time to take a peek. He walked up to the desk still glancing out the door. When he got to the desk, he didn't touch the notebook but angled his head so he could read the words on the cover.

H.Y.

AKA

WORDSMITH

## 10: HARVIS

*Wordsmith? What does that mean?* One more time Naz glanced out the open door. Curiosity got the best of him. He threw caution to the wind and opened the notebook with his free hand. But he still didn't pick it up. To his amazement, they weren't class notes at all but words—words on every line on every page it seemed. He continued to turn the pages, but there was nothing about health or any other school subject for that matter. And they weren't just words, but possibly songs, poetry, or some code or cipher. He stopped and decided to read:

> Too many atrocities being committed with extreme velocity
>
> They're steady choosing the corners instead of varsity
>
> In describing our city, you could call it larceny
>
> And have a strong point like archery
>
> To look into the skies and see a halo with no glow

Is to look into my eyes and see an angel with no soul

A tough Exclave to escape

The best place is where they educate

So this is where one meditates

They dare to break focus when one concentrates

These hands I'm quick to demonstrate

No heat on this waist, just cold looks on this face

Nothing but coldness from this race, so boldness is our place

An exiled Young, Wordsmith, they wish to harness in darkness

But this image can't be cropped 'cause this is the last harvest...

From out of nowhere, the spiky-haired boy appeared. He came face-to-face with Naz, grabbing Naz's wrist with one hand and slamming the book closed with the other. Naz found himself in a face-off, a stare-down. He tried feebly to release himself from the boy's hold on him, but it was futile. The boy's grip remained extremely tight, and Naz knew if he wanted to break free he would have to exert himself and then a struggle would likely ensue. He decided to defuse the situation with some light humor.

"Take it easy, Robin. Back up. Superman doesn't have a side-kick," Naz said jokingly. The boy didn't say a word. His expression didn't change, nor did his grip on Naz's wrist. As Naz looked at the boy, he thought he saw something in and around the boy's eyes that reminded him of—himself, something recognizable that he couldn't quite put his finger on. Like two boxers in a prizefight at center ring they stood toe-to-toe locked in an intense, but familiar stare. Naz saw a fight coming, and his smile faded to nothing. It had been a long day, and he'd had enough. Naz didn't know if he could fight, but they were both about to find out.

"Let 'em go, Harvis," Fears said calmly, as he entered the room and sat in the chair behind his desk. The boy immediately let go of Naz's wrist, while never taking his eye off Naz and never changing his expression. Naz turned to look at Fears.

"My guys, my guys," Fears laughed. "Good to see you getting acquainted. Mr. Young takes his work seriously, Mr. Andersen ... very seriously. Maybe you should, too."

Naz looked back at Harvis and replied, "Yes, Mr. Fears." Figuring that was his cue, Naz gathered himself and headed toward the door.

"And Mr. Andersen," Fears called.

Naz turned in the doorway. Harvis was still staring at him, expressionless.

"True vision goes beyond what the eye can see. If you ever wanna talk about how you got that nice little trophy," Fears said, pointing to Naz's neck, "you know where to find me."

Naz nodded and continued out of the classroom.

ONCE OUTSIDE, NAZ blew a sigh of relief. As he walked, he scanned the different clusters of students that had congregated on the school grounds. He checked the time on his phone. He had a few minutes.

*What was that all about, H.Y?* He worked it out in his head from what Fears had said. *H ... Y ... Harvis Young AKA Wordsmith, just cold looks on my face,* he remembered reading. *Harvis got that right*—a cold look indeed, colder than any he had ever seen before, but again, familiar.

Naz could still feel where Harvis had grabbed him round the wrist. He flexed his hand back and forth and then round and round without thinking about it. But his wrist wasn't heavy on his mind; his mind was somewhere else, on something else. He was looking for someone. In his search, he ended up walking around the entire school.

In his realm of reality, surviving the first day of school meant he successfully made it through a whole day—*and what a day it was!*

A lanky boy from Fears' class half-stood/half-sat on a bike, trying frantically to hide his bicycle helmet before anyone could see it. He attempted to stuff the helmet into a backpack that was already bursting at the seams. Naz laughed. The boy wouldn't have been so obvious, except that he was so freakishly tall, taller than any boy Naz had ever seen—*almost as tall as Fears.* The boy stopped and smiled at Naz—*for too long,* and Naz looked away.

A group of smaller kids horsed around on the lawn, and moments later a groundskeeper chased the little rascals away—*sixth-graders.* Naz shook his head. One of the kids pointed at Naz and made a stabbing motion. They all looked at Naz, taking a pause from their merriment. *He must have been one of the kids walking by and pointing this morning.* Naz didn't pay any of it much mind. He was on a more important mission—*she has to be out here.* It seemed like all the students were. *Then again I could have missed her while I was inside fooling around with Harvis and Fears.* After searching the entire perimeter of the building and coming up empty, he started to wonder if she even existed. *Maybe she didn't. What if I'm getting worse?* For the first time he had heard voices twice in one day, and maybe now he was hallucinating, too. *That would be bad.*

His phone buzzed in his pocket. It was a text from Meri.

> Pick me up @ 6 I'm stayin 4 chess club

He smiled and sent back:

> Take it easy on dem lil kids

She sent back:

> Absolutely, jus like I do u :p

Naz laughed and put his phone back in his pocket. He was still thinking about the girl, or whatever it was in the hallway saying, *"Come with me"* and *"Wait for me."*—*The girl* ... He didn't even know her name.

He remembered Harvis' words, *"look into the skies and see a halo with no glow"*—*maybe it was an angel.* He laughed. Meri believed in angels, but he wasn't so sure.

He finally stopped walking and looked around again. The students were much more scattered now, and it was evident he wouldn't find her, at least not today. He thought about going around one more time just to be sure and then abandoned the idea. He realized he was obsessing and let it go.

Not wanting to think about what had happened that morning, he took a different route when he left Lincoln, one that wouldn't take him where Ham had gotten stabbed. He grimaced. He would not again tread on that now unholy ground. But it didn't matter. It was as if his thoughts brought his fears into existence, and the boys from earlier that morning were now before him. Only they hadn't spotted him yet, and before they could, he ducked behind an abandoned house that had boards covering the windows.

There were abandoned houses all over the Exclave. Some of them were just about ready to collapse. There were at least two on the block where he lived. Naz was always amazed at the beautiful graffiti that seemed to appear on the abandoned houses overnight like magic. He also knew that in those same abandoned houses all manner of crimes took place, so usually, he made it a practice to steer clear of them.

Today he would find refuge behind this abandoned house and watch in dread as the two boys walked by. Part of his dread was based on a sudden flashback of the bloody nose the huskier boy had received courtesy of a vicious elbow from Ham. The boy's shirt was now clean. *He must've changed his shirt, too.*

Naz waited until he was sure the two boys were blocks away and going in the opposite direction. Then, he began to run, slowly at first, but gradually, he picked up the pace and ran faster. He loved to run. *I have two hours before I pick up Meri from school. It's time to make money.* On to the Market Merchants, he ran.

# II: THERAPY

As Naz sat back in the big La-Z-Boy chair, he thought about how much more comfortable this place was than the last place he had gone for therapy. Although he had moved four different times since coming to the Exclave, this was only the second therapist he'd seen. He started seeing her about a year after his mother died and had been having regular sessions with her for over a year.

The first week of school had come and gone. With the exception of that first day, the rest of the week had been uneventful. Even though Naz still hadn't talked to Ham, he did call his mother. She informed him that Ham was doing fine and would be back to school in a few weeks. She wanted Naz to know their family was grateful to him for being there when Ham had gotten stabbed. Naz couldn't help but wonder what story Ham had told his mother about what had happened that day.

Considering all that had happened on that first day of school, Naz was feeling pretty good about himself. Except for a few whispers and funny looks from his classmates after hearing his name during roll call, he had managed to accomplish his goal of staying invisible at Lincoln. He had even managed to stay under the radar of Fears.

But he had yet to find the girl. He scanned every table at lunch every day. He made a habit of walking around the entire building after school—sometimes more than once. He even took a chance by asking to be excused to go to the bathroom in Fears' class, not once but twice in the first week. He asked to leave about the same time he had seen her in the hallway on that first day. But still, there was no sign of her. He thought he might ask another student about her, but other than Ham, he didn't know anyone else at Lincoln. That was the downside of keeping to himself. He even considered talking to Harvis about her but abandoned that idea with the quickness.

As he waited patiently for his therapist to come in, he looked at all of the pictures on the walls in the cozy office—something he did weekly. Some of the pictures were actually paintings. *They must be famous psychiatrists.* He always told himself he would ask Dr. Hornbuckle when she came in, but he always seemed to forget.

Naz didn't care much for his first therapist. He was a mean old man who always insisted on calling Naz by his given name, even though Naz made it clear he didn't like it. He talked only about serious things that Naz wasn't interested in like the voices, sleepwalking, and his mother's death. He hated going to therapy back then.

But he liked Dr. Hornbuckle because they always talked about whatever he wanted to talk about. She told him she had a son just about his age and once brought one of her son's video games to a session, and they played the whole hour. Naz also thought she was pretty and looked forward to seeing her every Friday after school. Dr. Hornbuckle was the closest thing Naz had to a mother now, and he told her almost everything.

He was trying to decide whether or not to tell her about the voices. Up until a few days ago, it had been two months since he had heard them. Before that, when he had heard the voices, he kept it to himself. He had initially told Dr. Hornbuckle it had been almost a year since he had heard them. But now they were back. What bothered him most was that he had heard them twice in one day.

Early in their sessions, Dr. Hornbuckle told Naz that she could prescribe some medication to prevent him from hearing the voices. Meri brought home a book from the library once that said people diagnosed with schizophrenia often exhibited auditory hallucinations and paranoia. To Naz, the word schizophrenia meant crazy, and no one was going to tell him he was crazy—besides he wasn't about to take any medication. To Naz, drugs were drugs, and they were all bad.

From that point on, Naz decided he would just stop telling people, even his therapist, he heard voices. *But now, twice in one day and added to that I might be seeing things. Maybe I do need medication.* He pushed the thought out of his mind altogether. If there was one thing he knew, it was that the voices only came when he was angry, scared, or excited, all of which he believed were under his control.

Naz felt divided. Part of him wanted to tell Dr. Hornbuckle, and another part of him thought he shouldn't. He decided to play a game. If she asked him about the voices, he would tell her; if she didn't, he would keep it to himself. He figured he'd leave it to chance. She hadn't asked about the voices in quite a while, so he thought the odds were in his favor she wouldn't ask today either.

The wound on his neck was healing, but it also preoccupied him. He had forgotten to wear a bandage, and it was all he could do to keep from picking at it.

"Hello, Naz!" Dr. Hornbuckle said as she walked into the office. "I see you've made yourself at home."

# 12: DR. GWEN

D r. Guinevere Hornbuckle was statuesque, tall, and shapely. She was a middle-aged widow who always wore her hair in a bun and usually dressed in a casual two-piece pantsuit. She finished off her attire with a pair of running shoes. The running shoes always seemed out of place to Naz, but at the same time, they made him feel comfortable with Dr. Hornbuckle. He was comfortable with her from the first day he met her. She also carried a briefcase, which always caught Naz's attention because she never failed to have something inside of it for him.

"Good afternoon, Dr. Hornbuckle." He fidgeted.

"Dr. Hornbuckle, huh? Why so formal, Naz? You must have something good to tell me this week."

"Sorry, Dr. Gwen. Not really."

As she began to sit down in the chair directly across from him, she immediately saw the wound on his neck. She dropped her briefcase and moved toward him to investigate.

"Oh, my God! What happened?"

Naz had already leaned back in the chair, which made it easier for Dr. Gwen to tilt his head further back to see his neck. He had managed to conceal the wound from Miss Tracey all week, which wasn't difficult since she paid him and Meri little attention. But he forgot Dr. Gwen would most assuredly see his wound right away. It didn't matter. He had planned to tell her everything, except about the voices.

He actually looked forward to getting the news off his chest. Other than the police officer at the scene and Meri, he hadn't told anybody what had happened that day. Naz realized that if he told Dr. Gwen what happened, it would invariably lead her to ask about the voices. The odds were no longer in his favor.

"Well, I was sort of in a fight ... I guess."

"Sort of ... with who?" she asked, still standing over him and examining his neck. "Let me guess ... that Hector Martinez boy, right?"

"I wasn't in a fight with Hector."

"But it did have something to do with him, didn't it?" She asked, shaking her head.

Naz blinked.

"I knew it. I've never met that boy, but from all you've told me about him, I *knew* he was trouble." She finally sat down across from him. "Well, tell me what happened." She continued shaking her head while she pulled a notepad from the side of her briefcase.

Naz sat up in the chair. He started from the beginning: when he had met Ham that morning on the street. To his surprise, he enjoyed himself. It felt like he was telling a great, exciting tale. It felt like a Western again. He didn't leave out any details, except the voices. For the first time, he felt excitement when he thought about what had happened. He finished with an exhilarating exhale, his eyebrows raised.

"My goodness!" she said. "That's terrible!" Then, she paused for a moment and continued. "Yet, you seemed to enjoy it ... and that worries me because that's not like you ... not like you at all."

*She's right! What am I thinking*? It was the worst thing he had ever experienced, and now he was enjoying his reenactment of the events. He was embarrassed. "I'm sorry. You're right. It was terrible ... the worst thing I've ever been through. But I guess now that it's over, it doesn't seem real anymore. There's no fear ... no anger, just excitement."

"You don't have to apologize. What you feel is normal and part of being human. We all have a dark side that we struggle to keep concealed or caged every day. We seek the light, but usually, it's just before being consumed by the darkness. It's almost like a hero being taken to his limit by a villain. But in the end, we always root for the hero."

"That's deep. Are you saying it's the darkness that makes us who we are ... that defines us?"

"Not exactly, Naz, but don't be afraid to embrace it ... the darkness. It's an important part of you. Good and evil are two sides of the same coin. How we view and interpret good will always be colored by our emotions, tempered by our individual perceptions of evil, and based on our experiences."

Naz made a gesture with his hand, swishing it over the top of his head. "I think you just about lost me, Dr. Gwen."

"What I'm saying is I believe you're going to be fine. You have some conscience about what happened, and that tells me you'll be OK. What about your friend? I assume from your attitude that he's going to be OK as well."

"Yeah, his mom said he'll be back to school in a few weeks."

"Thank goodness for that. Now ... I heard you mention fear, anger, and excitement."

*Uh-oh, here it comes.* Dr. Gwen was sharp; she didn't miss a thing. The sequence of events he had revealed to her had brought her to a logical conclusion.

PART TWO
**DURATION**

## IN THE PAST...

C ory arrives at the podium to a standing ovation. "Thank you. *Merci.* Thank you," says Cory as he leans into the microphone. He smiles and nods in humble appreciation. With no cessation of applause, Cory raises his arms as a signal for the audience to stop clapping.

As the applause wanes and the many in attendance take their seats, one voice from the middle of the auditorium calls, "*We love you, Dr. Andersen.*"

"I love you, too," says Cory, laughing shyly.

There is a short silence as Cory, with his head down, gathers himself. Even though this scene is nothing new to him, he has never quite grown accustomed to the fuss made over his accomplishments. He is taken aback by the audience's response. The reception is more than he expected. He was just doing what came naturally, as a bird would take flight.

As he looks up, his expression is sober. "Again, thank you. You are too kind. Let me start this evening by giving credit where credit is due. You applaud me for all that I am, but I submit to you, here and now, that I am nothing ... nothing without the person that stands beside me." With his open hand, he gestures toward Camille and beckons her to step onto the stage and be recognized.

She shakes her head, waves him off, and mouths the refusal, "no," shyly to Cory.

"Come on, honey," he says. His hand covers the microphone so the audience won't hear while he continues to beckon her with his open hand.

Knowing, as with all things, he will not give up, she concedes and readies herself to walk onto the stage.

Cory proclaims, "Ladies and gentlemen, my all ... my everything ... my beautiful wife, Camille."

The audience applauds as Camille begrudgingly takes three steps onto the stage, gives a forced smile, a slight bow and then steps gracefully back into the wings of the stage. She gives Cory a dirty look when she is sure the audience cannot see her.

"My friends, I think that little stunt may have landed me a trip to the doghouse tonight," Cory says, and the audience laughs along. "But there's more! There is someone else to whom I am also indebted, someone I've known for a long time ... in fact, as far back as I can remember. You know him by his *nom de voyage*, the name under which he travels ... Cory Anders!"

He points to the back of the auditorium where there is a resounding boom, resembling the sound of cannon fire. The startled audience turns in surprise to see the auditorium doors opening to reveal none other than Dr. Cornelius Andersen, only he has changed. He sports a cream-colored, long-sleeved, collarless shirt and a matching pair of tailored pants that seem to shimmer under the houselights as he enters the auditorium.

The audience responds with gasps and murmurs, as they turn to look back and forth from the stage where Cory had stood mere seconds earlier, to the rear of the auditorium where he now appears dressed in starkly different attire.

Some begin to clap, but he raises his hand to stop them. As he makes his way toward the stage, he stops and greets a few of his colleagues and friends with a handshake here, a hug there, and a few friendly touches on the shoulder. He even introduces the president of the university. It is not until then that people in the audience begin to wonder how they can hear Cory. He has no microphone and to those close enough to see, there is nothing clipped to his shirt. Yet, they can hear him as clear as if he is sitting right next to them in the auditorium. The sound is even better than when he spoke at the microphone on stage.

"A trick?" asks Cory, as he slowly walks toward the stage. "No ... magic? It sounds so much better. And better still, an illusion? Now you see me, now you don't ... the sound of my voice coming from nowhere ... everywhere. But you believe just the same, don't you? Because you see it with your own eyes, hear it with your own ears. Toddlers learn to walk, and later as small children, ride bicycles, mainly because they believe. They believe because they have proof, provided by examples: people all around them walking and riding bicycles.

Conversely, as they get older they learn limitations: what they *cannot* do ... not based on their potential abilities, but another's lack of expectations and/or belief system. So, it really boils down to what we believe then. Doesn't it? The greatest Master taught us, 'what things soever ye desire, when ye pray, believe that ye receive them, and ye shall have them.'"

As he approaches the front of the stage, he lifts his hand, and dramatic music begins to play. As he lowers his hand, a large screen slowly comes down from the ceiling over the stage. The screen seems to move as if it is controlled directly by the movements of Cory's hand. It doesn't appear to be supported or suspended by anything other than the air itself, and its appearance elicits gasps and murmurs from the audience once more.

"You have to excuse the theatrics please, but I just love the roar of the crowd, the smell of the greasepaint, and I have a flair for the dramatic," says Cory.

Once the screen is in place, he faces the audience, raises his hands again, and asks, "Do you believe?" He snaps his fingers, and the lights go out.

# 13: THE VOICE

## PRESENT DAY...

What about the voices? Did you hear any during your encounter?" asked Dr. Gwen.

Naz smiled and shifted in his seat.

"Don't worry; I won't be prescribing any medication today."

"I ... I did, but not just during the fight, I-I heard 'em again at school, too."

Dr. Gwen suddenly came alive. She sat up in her chair. For the first time in a long time, she was genuinely excited, and it confused Naz. "Don't misunderstand my enthusiasm, Naz. I don't mean to sound excited that you've heard voices again, but understand that if we are to address and hopefully solve these so-called 'problems' that you have, then we need specific examples of what they are, and today it seems we have them."

"OK," Naz reluctantly agreed.

"Do you remember what the voices were saying?"

"Pretty much."

"I'm listening."

"The voice said, 'He's mmaaad and ... He's scared,' and 'He doesn't understand us.' It said, 'You can't fight,' and 'You better not run.' And, 'U...U...Únete a nosotros ...'"

"*Únete a nosotros?* The voice said *únete a nosotros?*"

"Well, the voice didn't say that, but one of the boys did. Do you know what it means?"

"It's Spanish for 'Join us,' Naz, now stay focused. What else did the voices say?"

"Sorry, Doc. It kept saying, 'You're gonna die, oh my God,' and 'blood.' And then it seemed to repeat after me, 'Somebody call an ambulance.'"

By now Dr. Gwen had put on her glasses and was writing feverishly away in her notebook. When Naz saw Dr. Gwen with her glasses on, his thoughts drifted immediately to the drinking fountain and the mysterious girl.

"Naz!" she said, bringing him back to reality. "What about the second time at school? Tell me about those."

Naz paused and then smiled shyly. There was an uncomfortable silence.

"Was it a girl, Naz?"

*How embarrassing! How could she know that?*

"If you're wondering how I knew, it's because we already know that the voices are triggered by emotions ... strong emotions. We've already dealt with the anger and the fear. Hmmm ... let me see. It was the first day of school for an eighth-grade boy with hair starting to grow on his chin. What else could I infer but an even stronger emotion ... love? Besides, you forget, I have a son. John is just about your age."

Naz's fingers automatically went up to touch his chin where hair had begun to grow. He didn't know whether to laugh out loud or ask to be excused to conceal his embarrassment.

"So, tell me all about it," she continued with a calming smile.

Naz told Dr. Gwen about the girl at the drinking fountain and how he stood on guard at the girls' bathroom and waited for her return. He gave her animated version using his hands to show how she appeared from nowhere and disappeared the same way. He was openly frustrated about not being able to find her since. Then, he told her about the voices as she continued to write.

"Naz, could it be that the voices you hear are likely you talking to yourself and that you externalize them as coming from somewhere else?"

Naz thought back—*at the drinking fountain the voice said, "What are you looking at?"* He tilted his head and looked puzzled. "I guess ... I do hear words that I'm thinking." As Naz thought further, he added, "But there are times when I hear words that I'm not thinking at all, and the voices are as clear as if someone is actually talking to me. We both keep saying voices, Dr. Gwen, but it's never voices, plural. There's only one voice, always the same voice."

"What do you hear, Naz? What voice ... whose voice?" She continued writing in her notebook.

"I don't know. I don't recognize the voice. I don't think I've heard it before. I can't explain it," Naz said as he began to sit up. He was getting louder and noticeably frustrated. "But somehow it is familiar."

"Maybe it's from your past, a voice from before you came to live with your mother." Dr. Gwen had a hunch and habit of never holding back when something came to her. "Your father, Naz, could it be your father's voice that you hear?"

"I don't know!" Naz raised his voice. He was now sitting straight up, holding his head in his hands. "I have no memory of him. You know that, Doc. I don't know what he sounded like or looked like." Naz stood up and paced around the room. "I've never even seen a picture of him. No one has ever shown me even a picture of my dad," he continued as if just realizing that fact.

"I think that's enough for today." Dr. Gwen took off her glasses.

Naz stopped pacing and looked at the clock on the wall. There was more time left in his session, and he valued his time with Dr. Gwen, so he calmed himself and sat back down. "I'm OK, Dr. Gwen."

"So tell me about this girl." She put her glasses back on.

Naz knew Dr. Gwen wasn't finished, and he figured she decided to change the subject and would come back to her theory at a later date. "There's not much to tell. I don't know her name or who she is, and I haven't seen her since that first day of school."

Naz looked at Dr. Gwen. He could tell she was still contemplating the origin and possible causes of the voice.

She finished jotting down a few notes and then looked up at him and said in an assuring tone, "I'm sure she'll turn up again. Is there anything else you'd like to talk about?"

"I have been sleepwalking again."

"Tell me about it."

"First, there was my dream." He was dying to tell Dr. Gwen about his dream. There was one good thing about the incident that morning in the Exclave; it seemed to burn the images of his dream in his mind.

Dr. Gwen resumed taking notes as Naz continued.

"I was trapped in my bathroom and couldn't get out. It seemed like there was a tornado coming and things were floating in mid-air ... the toothpaste ... the soap ... *me*! I could hear my mother on the other side of the bathroom door, but I couldn't make out what she was saying. The floor gave way, and while I was falling, I saw seven people. Then, I woke up. That morning, Miss Tracey found the bathroom a mess and said that I had been sleepwalking again. But there were things out of place in the bathroom that I never touched in my dream. How can that be, Dr. Gwen?"

"Who were the seven people?"

"I don't know. They were more shadows than anything."

"I've read somewhere that dreams can either remind you of your destiny or warn you of your fate. And I'm afraid that's about as much as I have, Naz. Dream research is a very complex and controversial field, and more to the point, it's not my field. As far as your sleepwalking is concerned, as I've said before, at your age, it's not uncommon. It may increase slightly in the next year as you go through puberty and then gradually decrease thereafter."

Naz heard the words but wasn't listening to Dr. Gwen's prognosis about his sleepwalking. He was more interested in what she might have to say about his dream, so he decided to come from a different angle. "Meri says that something big is about to happen in my life, that the things floating all over the place mean I've lost control, and that being trapped in the bathroom symbolizes my inadequacy to deal with the situation."

"Inadequacy?" Dr. Gwen said, laughing. "That sounds like a fine interpretation to me. I'll second that opinion. That's my little counselor. How is she anyway ... Miss Firecracker?"

"She's fine." He was hoping for more from Dr. Gwen about his dream, but it was evident he wasn't going to get it.

"That reminds me. I have something for you ... actually for Meri." She put her briefcase on her lap, opened it, and pulled out an envelope. "This is the first step." She handed Naz the envelope. "It's up to her now to do her best, and from what I know about little Miss Meridian Slaughter, she'll have no trouble making the grade." She paused to make sure she had Naz's full attention. "Naz, you do know that International Academy is a boarding school, right? If she scores high enough, there are scholarships out there that would provide her full tuition, as well as room and board for the next seven years."

Naz stood up with a look of excitement on his face. "I didn't know that. She'll score high enough." He looked at the thick envelope made of light green parchment. It had a raised crest with a large "I" and "A" in emerald green Old English style letters on the flap, but it wasn't sealed. Naz traced the crest lightly with his fingers. He smiled as he read the address.

MERIDIAN LIBERTY SLAUGHTER
C/O DOCTOR GUINEVERE HORNBUCKLE
15086 STANSBURY CIRCLE
BROOKESIDE VILLAGE, IL

"It is of the utmost importance that you be there on time—no, early, Naz. If you are even one second late, the doors will be closed and locked. She will not be admitted, and there will be no second chance. Do you understand?" Dr. Gwen asked with her eye trained on him.

"I understand. I will have Meri there at least an hour early, Dr. Gwen."

"Good, I knew you'd say that." She paused and then continued, "Naz, has anyone ever witnessed, or actually saw you sleepwalking—moving something while you were sleeping, picking up something ... anything at all?"

"Well, when I dreamed about the tornado and being trapped in the bathroom, Meri said she got up when she heard me sleepwalking. But she said by the time she got to the bathroom, I was already back in my bed asleep. So, no, I don't think so, never."

"Hmmm, interesting."

"Why?"

"No reason."

She was holding something back. Naz could sense it, but he knew he was just about out of time, and whatever she was thinking was probably going to have to wait. She reached into her briefcase one more time and pulled out a tarnished, odd-shaped skeleton key. She handed it to him.

"What is this?"

"A key," said Dr. Gwen, with a laugh.

Naz smiled as he stood up and prepared to leave. "OK, you got me, Doc, a key to what?"

"I was hoping you could tell me. Someone left it at the front desk for a Mr. Andersen. You're the only Mr. Andersen I know, so it must be for you."

He shook his head. "I don't know." He looked at the key, examining the shape and markings on it. The only person he was aware of that called him Mr. Andersen was Fears.

"Well, it's yours now. Maybe it'll come to you," she said.

He continued looking at the key, spinning it between his fingers as he walked to the door. There was something about it—*but then again maybe it's just an old key.*

"One more thing, Naz. What have you learned, if anything at all, from your little exploit with your friend, Hector?"

He stopped in the doorway and looked down for a second and then back up at her and replied, "To go my own way."

She smiled. "That's right, Naz, to go your own way. In the end, every man ... and woman must go his or her own way. You have to choose what's most important to you, prioritize and then conduct yourself accordingly ... and the next time you hear the voice, Naz, don't just hear ... try listening. If you don't like what it's saying, take a deep breath, calm down, and I promise you, it'll go away."

He smiled, nodded, and headed out the door.

# 14: THE MARKET MERCHANTS

Dr. Gwen left Naz with a lot to consider. Who would leave him a key? What did it unlock? What did it mean? Could it be Fears? And why would she bring up his father? That had always been a taboo subject, even with his first therapist, and here she was bringing him up out of nowhere and without hesitation. *Could it be his voice that I hear*? He made his way to the Market Merchants.

Meri played chess every day after school, which gave Naz time to run errands for the Market Merchants. He had started running errands for the Merchants shortly after his mother died, and now it had become quite lucrative.

The Market Merchants were a group of proprietors that, out of self-preservation, had agreed to work together in harmony. They needed to cooperate to survive the ominous presence of the mega discount department store chains that had sprung up. Through cooperation with one another, the Market Merchants managed to stave off the inevitable: eventual demise. They agreed not to undercut one another with lower prices and to charge the lowest possible amount for their goods, which in most cases was still not as low as what the Mega Chains charged for the same product. The owners sometimes decided this amount by unanimous vote, but more often by less formal means. They also agreed to keep the same hours, as well as the same weekend and holiday schedules.

These dynamics caused a war of commerce and economics between the Market Merchants and Mega Chains, and many felt there would never be peace again. The Mega Chain's primary tactic was to employ high-powered attorneys and cite collusion, while the supporters of the Market Merchants, favoring more guerilla-style warfare, resorted to arson and vandalism as their primary tools to voice their frustration. This volatile mixture added to the effect of the already nefarious Exclave.

**AFTER THE DEATH** of Naz's mother, things like music, computers, video games, and other luxuries were no longer available to Naz and Meri. Naz had discovered early on he and Meri would need more money than any foster parent or home would provide. He also knew that at only eleven years old, none of the Mega Chain discount department stores would consider giving him a real job, so he turned to the Market Merchants. One by one, they turned him down flat, telling him he was too young and that they would not hire him, not even for the most menial position.

Naz had just about given up hope when one day after school he walked into MeeChi's completely depressed and somewhat defeated. MeeChi's was owned and operated by Taverdae Tesla, a stern, bald, older man who stood barely five feet tall. MeeChi's was in Section 31, close to Naz's elementary school, which was just on the edge of Section 29—his section at that time. After school, Naz would often go to MeeChi's for a candy bar, soda, and chips. Of course, he could have found junk food in any of the markets on his way back home, but there was something else about MeeChi's that caught Naz's interest.

## 15: TONE

Just inside the door, on a perch, sat a medium-sized gray bird with a red tail named Antonio. Naz started going to MeeChi's right after he had arrived in the Exclave. Back then Mr. Tesla told Naz that Antonio was ten years old, the same age as Naz. Mr. Tesla had no idea the exact day Antonio hatched. About a year later, just before the accident, Naz went to MeeChi's with his mom and Meri on a rare occasion. Without Naz knowing, Mr. Tesla asked their mother Naz's birth date. A few weeks later, on his birthday, Naz happened into MeeChi's. Mr. Tesla handed him an official-looking document that read:

> Department of Health Vital Records
> Certificate of Live Hatching
> Species: African Grey Parrot
> Sex: Male
> Name: Antonio Warner Tesla
> Place: Penelope's Pet Palace
> Date of Birth: July 8th

There was an official-looking seal from the Illinois Department of Health at the bottom of the document. Naz became excited when he saw that Antonio had hatched on the same day he was born and then remembered he and Antonio were also the same age. Mr. Tesla told Naz he could keep Antonio's hatch certificate as a birthday present because it would just end up getting lost at Mee-Chi's anyway. From then on, Naz looked at the bird differently, as if they were connected in some way. Ever since then he had been drawn to Antonio.

Whenever someone walked into MeeChi's, Antonio usually said, *"Welcome to MeeChi's,"* but when Naz walked in, Antonio always seemed to say something different. Naz had heard that talking birds usually had a very limited vocabulary and only repeated what they heard if they heard something over and over again. Mr. Tesla told Naz that Antonio's species was the smartest of all birds on the planet. Naz swore to Mr. Tesla Antonio would say new things to him all the time that he never heard him say before.

A few months after the accident, Naz walked into MeeChi's feeling defeated. He had already asked Mr. Tesla for a job, and like all of the other Market Merchants, Mr. Tesla told him he was too young.

*"Seize the day, seize the day,"* said Antonio.

Naz, not thinking anything of Antonio's words, walked up to him, opened his hand, and presented the bird with two larger than average sunflower seeds. The bird took one seed in his beak and ate it. He took the other seed and dropped it in the small cup under him. Naz turned and walked down the aisle as he heard Antonio say, *"Thank you."*

Naz looked at all the merchandise as he tried to figure out a solution to his problem. He needed a job. Mr. Tesla had promised Naz he would give him a job when he turned twelve. But that was almost a whole year away, and Naz needed money now. He was tempted to run errands for the drug dealers, but he had promised his mother he would never resort to that. However, she was gone now, and he and Meri needed things, things they were used to having, things they couldn't do without.

Mr. Tesla, like all of the Market Merchants, stocked MeeChi's with the widest variety of goods that he could pack onto the shelves in his little store. From clothes to groceries, small appliances to toys, games, and computers, MeeChi's was bursting at the seams with goods. It was a combination of a large convenience store and a mini department store.

The biggest problem that MeeChi's faced, along with the other Market Merchants, was finding an efficient balance between the quantity of a specific product and a variety of different goods. They didn't have enough space to purchase and stock large quantities of goods like the Mega Chains and often found themselves out of stock of something that might be crucial to a loyal customer.

As Naz walked down an aisle, he continued to hear Antonio's words, "*Seize the day, seize the day.*" He could also hear Mr. Tesla one aisle over in the middle of an intense discussion with someone. He couldn't quite make out what was being said, but the other man was clearly upset, and Mr. Tesla was trying to explain something to him. Naz was curious, so he went to the next aisle where Mr. Tesla was talking to a man dressed in work clothes. Naz figured he wasn't eavesdropping; he was just someone shopping in the garden aisle and looking for a water hose right next to the two men engaged in a disagreement.

Mr. Tesla was trying to convince the man he would be getting a shipment in sometime soon that very day. It just hadn't arrived yet. The man was losing his patience, complaining this had happened too many times and not just at MeeChi's but with other Market Merchants as well. He said he was just about done supporting the Market Merchants and was threatening to take his business to Major General, one of the Mega Chain discount department stores. The man's business must have been landscaping—*or something like that.* Naz looked at the space on the shelf in front of the two men and then eyed the goods the man already had in his cart.

Naz could still hear Antonio at the front of the store; he was repeating, "*Seize the day, seize the day.*" These words in the back of Naz's mind finally came to the forefront and made sense. As the disgruntled and disgusted man headed to the checkout with the other things in his cart, Naz came up with an idea.

# 16: SEIZE THE DAY

**N**az didn't have a plan yet, only an idea and very little time, so he went to work. He carefully examined the space on the shelf where Mr. Tesla and the man had just been standing. The sticker on the shelf read:

Henzi's
GrubGone
Season-long Grub Killer
14.5 lbs.
$19.95

He read it several times so he wouldn't forget it and then quickly left MeeChi's and ran down the street. He still could hear Antonio's words in his mind—*seize the day, seize the day*. He said it aloud one more time to himself. "Henzi's GrubGone Season-long Grub Killer 14.5 lbs. $19.95."

Four blocks south and a half-mile away in Section 29 was Piccolo's, another market Naz frequented. As Naz ran, he formulated a plan. All the markets in that area sold the same goods and used the same suppliers. Naz liked playing the odds, and he figured the odds were in his favor that Piccolo's would have what MeeChi's did not.

Naz could run a mile in less than six minutes He had done so in school the year before. He would be back at MeeChi's before the man could complete his purchase. The only flaw in his plan was how he would pay for the grub killer. He didn't have any money. His only option was to steal the grub killer and somehow pay for it later.

He thought about what his mother had told him. *It's not always about right or wrong; sometimes it's about having a good reason,* and in his mind, this was as good a reason as any. He didn't have much time. He had to throw caution to the wind, trust his instincts, and get in and out in a hurry.

When he got to Piccolo's, he walked straight to where he knew the grub killer would be. His gamble paid off. As he predicted, the grub killer was there. He looked around. No one paid him any attention. He didn't think about the surveillance system. If someone there was watching, they could never catch him once he got outside and ran.

He picked up the grub killer, which weighed almost fifteen pounds, and walked to the door as if he had already paid for the item. When he got to the door, he backed out, turned around, put the bag on his shoulders, and took off. He never looked back. He was used to running with Meri on his shoulders, so the almost fifteen pounds felt like no weight at all for most of the half-mile run back.

When Naz got to MeeChi's, the muscles in his legs were on fire. Just before he walked in, he put the bag down, shook his legs out, and took another minute or two to dry his sweating face on his shirt. When he came in, he saw the man in work clothes at the register. The cashier was ringing up his items as he was placing them back into his cart for transport. Naz slipped in through one of the unused checkout aisles, went down one aisle, and came back up the next aisle as if he had come from the back of the store, all the while still catching his breath. He could faintly hear Antonio saying, *"Seize the day, seize the day."*

He approached the man from the rear and called to him to let him know he had forgotten something. The man saw the grub killer as Naz placed it on the counter for the cashier to ring up. Naz told him he had found the grub killer in the back. The man thanked Naz and complimented Mr. Tesla who was now assisting the cashier on a neighboring register. He wanted to let Mr. Tesla know how much he appreciated the staff at MeeChi's for their diligence. He then apologized for ever doubting Mr. Tesla's integrity and assured him he would not be taking his business over to Major General.

When the man left, Mr. Tesla took Naz down an empty aisle for a one-on-one. He knew Naz didn't get the grub killer from the back because in MeeChi's there was no back. Mr. Tesla continued by expressing his gratitude to Naz for preventing the loss of a loyal customer to one of the Mega Chains. He handed Naz twenty dollars for what he called "Naz's troubles" and then another twenty dollars for what he called "unfinished business." He told Naz to pay for the grub killer wherever he got it from, and he would see him the next day about a job.

Before Naz left MeeChi's, he pulled a handful of sunflower seeds out of his pocket, put them in Antonio's cup, and thanked him. Antonio didn't respond. Naz thanked him one more time, but there was still no response. He smiled at the bird and then walked out the door. As he was leaving, he heard Antonio say, "*You're welcome,*" and laughed.

He couldn't remember ever feeling so good, at least not since his mother had died. He had forty dollars in his pocket—more than he ever had before—and he had prevented the loss of a loyal customer to the Mega Chains. In the process, he had earned himself a job at his favorite market: MeeChi's—*all in a day's work.* He walked down the street with his head held high.

Then it hit him. His day's work was only half complete. That was the easy part. How would he square the situation at Piccolo's? He didn't even know the owner there. Maybe he could get Mr. Tesla to call. No, he got himself into this, so he had to get himself out of it.

Maybe he wouldn't do anything. It looked like he had gotten away with stealing the grub killer. If he could just lay low for a few weeks or even a month and not go into Piccolo's it would all blow over, and it would be just like it never happened.

But Naz would know. Somewhere along the way he had developed a conscience. If he didn't go back to Piccolo's, he would be no more than a common thief and no better than the drug dealers on the street. He finally decided on just handing twenty dollars to a cashier at Piccolo's as if he had found it near the register. That way it would be as if it had never happened, and he would've paid his debt. He could live with that.

It was the slowest he ever walked in his life, but he seemed to get to Piccolo's faster than when he had run there almost an hour earlier. When Naz walked into Piccolo's, it was just as it was before with no one noticing him. The store was half full, and everyone seemed fairly busy, so he figured his quick fix would be a piece of cake.

He stood in line as if he was going to purchase something. He thought to make it look legitimate he should buy something, so he picked up a candy bar while he was in line. The closer he got to the cashier, the hotter he felt all over. His heart seemed to beat even faster than it did when he was running—*but how can that be?* He heard the voice mixed in with all the voices around him.

Just before Naz got to the cashier, he separated the two twenties that were in his pocket. He put one back in his pocket and palmed the other one. When he got to the register, he handed the candy bar to the cashier, and she rang it up. He pulled the twenty out of his pocket and gave it to her. While she was making change, Naz dropped the other twenty on the floor. Just as he was about to reach down, a man in back of him told him he had dropped his money. Confused, Naz picked up the money and handed it to the cashier, while she tried to give him the change for the other twenty.

Finally, the cashier looked up at him and recognized that he had just been there an hour before. He was caught. She pushed a button on the other side of the register, and in what seemed like seconds a tall man came from a booth near the front of the store. He had dark eyes and dark, long, stringy hair.

Naz's greatest success had just turned into his most embarrassing failure. He was about to pay for the grub killer all right, with his freedom. He wouldn't need that job anymore because he was going to jail, and Meri would be alone. The walk to the booth was even longer than the walk back to Piccolo's as people began staring and pointing at the boy who was caught stealing a bag of grub killer. He actually felt relieved. It was over now. He was a criminal, a juvenile delinquent, something Meri's father had told him he would end up being anyway.

In the booth, the stringy-haired man picked up the phone and dialed. Naz was about to have his third run-in with the police, and he was fairly confident this third time would be no charm. Instead, it would be the third strike in a game he had played well but ultimately lost.

Suddenly the man stopped dialing and looked at Naz suspiciously. He was confused. He wanted to know why an eleven-year-old boy, or anyone else for that matter, would steal a bag of grub killer and then come back an hour later with the money to pay for it. He gave Naz one chance to explain. Naz had nothing to lose, so he told the truth.

The man put the phone down for a minute and then picked it up again. He called Mr. Tesla to confirm what Naz had said. The man had a long conversation with Mr. Tesla. Naz remembered hearing words like resourceful, impeccable, and altruistic, words he wanted to look up in a dictionary when he got home or back to school.

In the end, four of the Market Merchants: MeeChi's, Piccolo's, Bellarusso's, and Mercado's hired Naz as a link to ensure the Merchants stayed supplied by sharing resources daily and settling up once a week. They employed Naz between two and three hours a day after school and Saturdays on an on-call basis. For Naz's part, he received significantly more money than he would have if he had worked for only one of the Merchants, and even then, he would've had to work more hours. The Market Merchants also paid for the use of two phones for him and Meri. And so the Merchants became an inseparable part of the world of Naz Andersen.

# 17: MR. TESLA & MEECHI'S

MeeChi's was more like a home to Naz than any of the foster homes in which he had lived, and Mr. Tesla was the closest thing to a father Naz had ever known or at least could remember. When Naz came in with the bandage on his neck, the tone of the argument between him and Mr. Tesla was more that of a father and son than an employer and employee.

While running his errands, Naz always made MeeChi's the first and last stop of the day. That way he could get a snack right after school or therapy, and often Mr. Tesla would treat him and Meri to dinner before they went home in the evening. Naz felt important at MeeChi's. Mr. Tesla trusted him with everything, which sometimes made the other employees jealous.

Like Piccolo's, MeeChi's had a large booth in the front of the store that was elevated. You could see almost everything in the store through a large two-way mirror. The booth was more like a room. There was a surveillance system of cameras that fed into ten monitors mounted on the wall next to the two-way mirror. There was a control panel just beneath them. Next to the wall, opposite the monitors were a refrigerator and conventional stove with a microwave oven on top. There was also a small television on a dresser. Next to the dresser was a desk. The booth also included a small cot. In the middle of the room was a small table with a worn picture in an old frame as its centerpiece.

The picture on the table was of a much younger Mr. Tesla with a full head of hair. He was standing next to a woman who was slightly taller than he was. The two looked happy and content, and Naz assumed the woman must have been Mrs. Tesla but was afraid to ask. The picture made Naz think of his mother and Dr. Gwen's loss and often put him in a somber mood. Whenever he sat at the table, he always sat with the picture facing away from him. But the picture had a purpose. Knowing it was there was a constant and stark reminder of the harsh realities of the Exclave, and every day it kept him mindful of what he faced in his world.

Dr. Gwen's words were still on Naz's mind when he walked into MeeChi's after his therapy session. He walked right past Antonio as the bird bobbed his head up and down in excitement.

*"Naz is here. Naz is here,"* said Antonio.

"Oh, hey, Tone," said Naz, looking back at the bird as he walked to the booth.

Tone didn't respond.

More often than not Mr. Tesla was busy on the store floor, checking inventory, greeting and attending to customers, or assisting employees. But when Naz arrived every day after school it was a safe bet he would find Mr. Tesla in the booth. In fact, Naz counted on it. When Naz walked in the booth today, Mr. Tesla was busy working at his desk.

Without even looking up, Mr. Tesla said, "And who are we today? Sam, Naz, or—"

"Naz, Mr. T," Naz replied, cutting Mr. Tesla off.

"And Mr. Tesla will do ... Naz," retorted Mr. Tesla. "And you need to teach that stupid bird of yours some manners."

"Mr. Tesla! He's not stupid, he's stubborn, and the last time I checked, on the certificate you gave me, his last name was Tesla."

"That can be easily rectified. He doesn't even greet the customers anymore. And what's with all those weird, new sounds he makes: a siren, a phone ringing, a dog barking? Last week several customers ran out of the store because they thought the smoke alarm went off, but it was only Tony. Did you teach him all that stuff?"

"Tone, Mr. Tesla ... Me? I can't make sounds like that."

"Tone, Tony, what's the difference? He won't answer to either one. Did you get my list today?" Mr. Tesla pulled a cell phone out of his pocket. He looked at the phone as if it were a foreign object and shook his head.

"Always do. You can trust the technology, Mr. Tesla. It works."

"These things are amazing." Mr. Tesla continued fiddling with the phone.

It was Naz's idea that all of the Market Merchants he worked for send him a list of the items they would be exchanging with one another in a text message. The Merchants would have the goods prepared for Naz to transport by the time he arrived. Depending on the size of the load, Naz would determine the mode and speed of transportation. The Merchants had surprised Naz with a brand new bike for Christmas two years ago, and he sometimes used this as well. But Naz's favorite mode was his legs and his favorite speed was running—fast.

Naz took off his backpack and slid it under the table.

"By all means, make yourself at home," said Mr. Tesla.

Naz smiled and looked down at the bundle on the floor next to the door. "Anything breakable?" asked Naz as he walked to the refrigerator.

"No, but still be careful. There are some small electronics."

Naz looked in the refrigerator and pulled out a red soda pop and a ham and cheese sandwich wrapped in clear paper. "Fuel."

"Don't be bashful; help yourself."

This had become their daily routine with only slight variations in the meal Mr. Tesla had prepared and their verbal jabs and pleasantries with each other. Naz sat on his preferred side of the table where he couldn't see the picture, unwrapped the ham and cheese sandwich, and ate.

"Any homework today?" asked Mr. Tesla.

"I suppose."

"Plan on doing it?"

"Maybe I will, and maybe I won't, depends on if I have time."

School came easy to Naz. It was boring to him. He hated it and did just enough to get by. He knew if he half-paid attention in class, did well on all his tests, quizzes, and classroom assignments, he would pass all of his classes, and that was good enough for him. To him, homework just wasn't a priority. Mr. Tesla, along with Dr. Gwen and all of Naz's teachers would always say Naz wasn't living up to his potential. Naz wondered, what was his potential? He barely knew who he was, how could he have any idea what or who he wanted to be. So he lived day-to-day, in the moment he liked to say. He didn't put much stock in structure or rules that he viewed were only there to constrain him.

Between running back and forth to school and running for the Market Merchants, Naz used up plenty of energy. But it didn't take him long to replenish his stores. He ate the ham and cheese sandwich in less than two minutes, put the bundle of goods on his back, and headed out of the booth with soda pop in hand.

"See you in about two hours, Mr. Tesla."

"Be careful, no more knife fights."

Naz gave Mr. Tesla a thumbs-up.

Before Naz left the store, he put some sunflower seeds in Tone's cup and bid the bird farewell. He waited for Tone's reply, but again the bird was silent. Naz chuckled.

Naz took different routes to the various merchants and never the same path twice in a row if he could help it. That way the gang leaders and drug dealers who tried to recruit kids his age to gang bang and sell drugs and anyone else who was interested in his affairs couldn't get a bead on him.

Naz's first stop was a half mile east into Section 29 where he would drop off and pick up at Piccolo's for Ibrahim Moussa, the tall, dark-eyed, stringy-haired proprietor who had first helped set up Naz's unique arrangement with the Market Merchants, now known as the Market Quadrumvirate. From there it was two miles north into Section 30 to Mercado's, owned and operated by the eccentric Mercel Cardonias, the most successful of the merchants in the Quadrumvirate. Next, Naz would take a break and pick up Meri from Higginbotham, which was about a mile-and-a-half southwest of Mercado's and a mile southeast of Bellarusso's, which was Naz's last stop before returning to MeeChi's.

# 18: BELLARUSSO'S

Bellarusso's was owned and operated by Richelle Bella and Frances Russo. Richelle and Frances had a special place in their hearts for Meri and wouldn't let Naz run errands there without her.

There were always two bundles packed when Naz arrived: one for him and a smaller one for Meri. And they always paid Meri instead of Naz. For all intents and purposes, it was Meri's account, and Naz was just there to help her. Naz didn't mind. He thought it was good for her. She now had her own money, and the responsibility made her even more mature than she already was.

But when Meri, Richelle, and Frances began to discuss the possibility of Meri making some shorter runs on her own, Naz made it clear that proposition was out of the question. Naz could take care of himself, but even in broad daylight, the Exclave was a no-win scenario for a nine-year-old girl carrying potentially valuable goods, commodities, and money on her person.

"WHAT TOOK YOU so long?" asked Meri as she stood on the school steps and removed her earbuds.

"This is the same time I got here yesterday," replied Naz.

"Right, late!"

"I thought I told you to wait ... *inside* the school."

"You did, but it's boring in there. There's nothing to do once chess club is over. It's more exciting out here."

"Yeah, that's what I'm afraid of."

From Higginbotham to Bellarusso's, Naz walked for the first time. The fifteen- to twenty-minute walk gave him and Meri a chance to talk about what had happened at school that day, Miss Tracey, and anything else.

Once Naz and Meri arrived at Bellarusso's, no matter where Richelle and Frances were in the store or what they were doing, they always found their way to the front. They were anxious to see Meri, give her a big hug, and ask her a series of questions. Naz didn't mind so much that they ignored him. What bothered him most was that it took so long. Naz had one rule for working for the Market Merchants, especially when Meri was with him. He had to be home before sundown; the Exclave was no place for two kids—or anyone else for that matter—to be at night.

When Naz and Meri walked into Bellarusso's, Frances was working one of the registers, as she often did. When she saw Meri, she ran over and greeted her with a big hug.

"How's my Firecracker?" Frances asked.

"Fine, Miss Russo, how are you?" asked Meri.

"Girl, I thought I told you to call me Miss Francy."

"You did. I just keep forgetting."

The customer at the register rolled his eyes and let out an audible sigh.

Moments later, Richelle appeared from nowhere, also giving Meri a big hug. "You guys are a little late," said Richelle as she looked at her watch.

"I told you," said Meri, looking at Naz with a sardonic grin.

The two ladies turned to see Naz as if they had just noticed him for the first time.

"Oh, I'm sorry, Naz, I didn't see you standing there," said Richelle.

"We should've known," said Frances. "It's always the weakest link," she continued referring to Naz in a half-joking manner. "We ladies have to stick together, you know." She winked at Meri.

Meri attempted to wink back.

The two ladies had been best friends as far back as they could remember. They started Bellarusso's with the insurance money Richelle received after her husband had been murdered over fifteen years ago. Frances never married. Between the two women, they had seven children—all boys and all working at Bellarusso's. It was no wonder they took such a liking to Meri.

"How was school today?" Richelle asked Meri.

"*Our* day was good," said Naz, before Meri could answer. "And I think *we* should all get back to work." He pointed to the gentleman who was just about ready to lose his temper at the register. "Because I wouldn't want to be *late* for *my* last delivery."

They all turned in surprise and looked at Naz. Frances walked back to her register to finish assisting her customer, all the while nodding her head in approval. Richelle and Meri stood with their mouths open. This breach of silence was a first. Naz usually never spoke up or out about anything.

"The silent soldier grows up," said Richelle. She reached behind the counter, pulled out a small bundle, and gave it to Meri. Then, she pulled an envelope from the pocket of her apron and handed it to Meri.

Naz reached behind the same counter and pulled out a larger bundle and put it on his back.

"Ready?" Naz looked at Meri.

She nodded.

"Remember, us ladies have to stick together," said Richelle.

Meri nodded again as she and Naz walked toward the door.

"Be careful," said Richelle.

Frances waved from her register as the two walked out waving goodbye.

"Wait!" said Meri as she set the bundle on the ground and put the envelope in her sock. "You should do that all the time," she continued, as she stood up and put the bundle on her back.

"Do what?" Naz asked.

"You know, talk up. Stick up for yourself."

"I always stick up for myself."

"No, you always stick up for me. There's a difference."

He thought about what she said and shrugged his shoulders. "Wanna run?" he asked.

"How fast?"

"That's up to you. But remember your heart condition."

He was trying to use reverse psychology to goad her into running, but it wasn't necessary. They both knew the doctor said running would make her heart stronger, and she enjoyed running almost as much as he did.

"Let's go," she said, ignoring him.

## 19: SPOOKED

**B**ack at MeeChi's, Mr. Tesla prepared hot turkey sandwiches with gravy and mashed potatoes for Naz and Meri. Meri ate almost as much as Naz did, and he wondered where she put it all. Afterward, Mr. Tesla let them have as much Neapolitan ice cream and chocolate cake as they could eat. Meri didn't have any homework due until Monday so the three of them played Scrabble and listened to Meri's favorite oldies radio station until Naz decided it was getting too late, and the sun would set on them. He wasn't going to let that happen. Naz thought it was a perfect end to a week that had started out to be the worst he ever remembered.

Naz put on his backpack and glanced through the two-way mirror. Standing at the register was someone he recognized. It was the husky boy with the Mohawk from the first day of school—the same one that had stabbed Ham. He was talking to the cashier and handed her something. "Mohawk" looked up at the two-way mirror, and for a moment Naz felt like Mohawk was looking at him. *But that can't be.* Naz had once been so intrigued by the mirror that he looked at the mirror side over and over again, never being able to see through to the other side. *It has to be my imagination.*

"Naz," Meri called.

Naz, frozen, continued to stare through the two-way mirror, barely aware of Meri's summons. A chill ran through him as he watched Mohawk walk away from the cashier and head to the door to meet the boy with the gruff voice that had cut Naz. There was also another boy with fiery red hair and freckles, but Naz didn't recognize him.

Mohawk, "Gruff," and "Red" teased Tone as Tone moved from side-to-side on his perch in a frustrated motion. Naz clenched his fists, but he didn't dare do anything but watch. Red kept putting his finger near Tone's beak. Tone turned his head to the side. Red had two symbols tattooed on his forearm. From where Naz stood, it looked like something wrapped around a sword and an eye. Mohawk and Gruff had the same symbols on their arms. There was a cracking sound of glass breaking, which brought Naz back to reality. The two-way mirror had somehow cracked leaving a thin line in the thick glass.

"Naz!" Meri called again.

"Huh?"

"Aren't you gonna answer Mr. Tesla?"

"I'm sorry, Mr. Tesla."

Mr. Tesla examined the unexplained crack in the two-way mirror while Meri looked through the mirror to see what had Naz so spooked. By then, Mohawk, Gruff, and Red had left the store. Naz breathed a sigh of relief.

"I wonder how that happened," said Mr. Tesla, examining the glass. "Tomorrow morning we're getting a big shipment in. If you and Meri would like to come by and help organize the shelves, you're more than welcome. We'll be here most of the day."

"Ooh, can we?" Meri asked Naz.

"I don't know. Don't you have a lot of homework?" asked Naz, trying to play the concerned parent. Truth be told, he was always looking for a good excuse to get out of Miss Tracey's house on the weekend.

Meri, in her best Naz imitation, said, "Maybe I do, and maybe I don't."

Mr. Tesla let out a roar of laughter that betrayed his small stature and startled both Meri and Naz.

That was good enough for Naz. "Looks like we'll be here," he said, as he and Meri joined in the laughter.

Before Naz left MeeChi's, he asked the cashier in private what Mohawk had said to her. She told him Mohawk was looking for him and then she handed him the note Mohawk had given her. It was still folded as if she hadn't read it. Before he joined Meri, who was at the door with Tone, he opened it to read:

## Join us or else!

## 20: THE HAVEN

On the way home, Naz didn't talk much. When Meri asked him questions, he only offered one-word responses. Just when he had put the incident on the first day of school behind him, there were those boys again, not just Mohawk and Gruff, but a third one as well. *What are those symbols on their forearms?*

All of a sudden it was clear to him. They were part of some gang, and they wanted him to join them. But why select him? He remembered what Fears had said about avoiding gangs at all costs, that gangs were for the weak-minded follower.

He remembered the promise he had made to his mother that he would never join a gang. But he didn't need Fears or his mother's words for that. He had no intention of ever joining a gang. He just didn't understand why they were so hell-bent on recruiting him. Would he have to watch his back on the street now? *Obviously, they'll be back, and when they come, I'll put my foot down and let them know I'm not interested. Like Dr. Gwen said, 'every man must go his own way.'*

When Naz and Meri got home, they went straight to his room. He had promised her all week he would play her in a game of chess when they got home on Friday. Meri was convinced that with what she had learned the first week of school in the chess club at Higginbotham, she could finally beat him.

"Don't take this personal," said Naz.

"Look!" said an agitated Meri as she pointed to his bedroom door.

There was the lock that Miss Tracey had promised but not on the inside of his door as Naz had anticipated. It was a large padlock on the outside of his door. Apparently, he was to be locked in his room at night to prevent him from sleepwalking around the rest of the house.

"That does it!" Meri said as she turned to walk down the hall.

Naz grabbed her by the arm before she could move. "What are you gonna do?" he asked.

Without a word, she snatched away from him, stormed down the hallway to Miss Tracey's bedroom, and forced her way through the closed door. Miss Tracey, who was in bed while watching television and talking on the phone, jumped up. She was wearing a nightgown and a scarf on her head. Meri stood inside the doorway with her hand on her hip.

"Can I call you back?" asked Miss Tracey of the person on the other end of the phone and then hung up. "Oh, no, you didn't. I thought I told you never to come in my room without knocking, little Miss—"

"I may be only nine years old, but even I know it's illegal to lock a kid in a room." Meri pulled her phone out and began to dial.

"Woosah," said Miss Tracey in a calm manner and then asked, "And just who do you think you're calling?"

"The Haven will want to know about this," said Meri to herself as she finished dialing and put the phone to her ear.

"Hang up that phone, you little brat!"

"My name is Meridian, and I'm not!" Meri put her free hand over her other ear and turned to the side.

"GIVE ME THAT PHONE!" yelled Miss Tracey at the top of her lungs.

"I won't!" said Meri in an insolent tone.

Miss Tracey lunged at Meri, who had now turned completely away from her. Miss Tracey grabbed her by the shoulders. "GIVE ME THAT PHONE!"

"No!" Meri was holding the phone with her arm extended to keep it out of Miss Tracey's reach.

The two began to tussle.

"LET ME GO!" yelled Meri.

"GIVE ME THAT PHONE!"

"Let ... her ... GO!" said Naz in a stern voice.

The two stopped and turned to see Naz standing in the doorway. Miss Tracey let go of Meri. Meri put the phone back to her ear.

"Hello, I'd like to report an incident of child abuse," said Meri to someone on the other end of the phone.

"OK," said Miss Tracey in a forced whisper.

"An address?" asked Meri into the phone.

"I said OK!"

"Can you hold on for a second?" asked Meri, again to the person on the other end of the phone. She covered up her phone's mouthpiece. "What?"

"I'll take off the lock."

"I'm sorry; I didn't hear you."

"I *said* ... I'll take the lock off."

Meri hung up the phone.

"But it goes back up tomorrow on the inside of the door," Miss Tracey added.

"We can live with that," said Meri, calming down immediately.

"Now get out of my room before I change my mind." Miss Tracey adjusted the scarf that had all but fallen off her head.

Naz and Meri hurried back down the hallway with smirks on their faces. Naz was barely able to contain himself. They waited until they heard Miss Tracey slam her door and then broke into laughter.

"Looks like we win," said Meri, laughing.

"I told you, you're gonna get us put out of here," Naz said through his laughter. "But thanks for sticking up for me."

"Somebody has to. Thanks for coming to my rescue in there ... my silent soldier," she said imitating a damsel in distress.

They both laughed again.

"Did you see the look on her face when you said, 'Let ... her ... go'?" Meri asked, lowering her voice to imitate Naz's voice.

"And The Haven? What was that?"

"Heck if I know. I just made it up."

"I'm still gonna kick your butt," said Naz playfully as he pulled the chess set from underneath his bed.

"In your dreams."

"Please, don't mention dreams." The two continued laughing.

## 21: SILENT SOLDIER

**N**az turned on the lights. He needed a distraction, a change of pace, something to keep his mind off the nightmare. It was a recurring dream that hadn't shown itself for months but had somehow crept back into his slumber this night with a vengeance. He had already woken from it once before only to return to the same scene, as if someone had pressed pause and then play when he fell asleep again. Now, to stay awake and force himself into a different state of mind, he decided to walk the hallways of Miss Tracey's and check on Meri.

He wasn't as good as Meri at keeping up with things, so he used a paper clip to attach the key right to the padlock itself on his door. That way he could easily find it when he needed to get out.

As he took the lock off his door and opened it, he looked back at the room that not so long ago had been empty. Now with the lock on his door and much-desired privacy, the empty nightstand was now home to not just a Bible, but a high-tech lamp given to him by Mr. Tesla—a lamp to read by if the spirit were ever to move him, though it rarely did.

He could now come home every day and improve his accuracy or just let off some steam by going for the bulls-eye on his dartboard, which hung on the wall opposite his bed. And there was the dusty, badly out-of-tune guitar he hadn't played in over a year. But he kept it out, leaning against the wall, just the same. It just felt so good to have things lying around, even if he didn't use them anymore. It felt like a bedroom again, his bedroom.

He looked at the calendar hanging next to the door. *Thank God it's Friday ... well, Saturday now.* It had been five weeks since school started, and after a shaky start, things were normal again. There was a big X that marked the calendar for today, this special Saturday. Today was the day Meri would take the entrance exam at International Academy. She had been interviewed at Dr. Gwen's office by a representative of the school the week before and felt good about it.

But there was no way to prepare for the test, no study guide and no cheat sheet, only a list of words Dr. Gwen had given him—words like classify, construct, and identify. She also gave Meri a word search puzzle and two crossword puzzles containing the words. She told Naz the words would be useful, and that they would apply to any test. Naz didn't even know anyone who had ever taken the test before. But Dr. Gwen assured him Meri would do well, and there was no reason to doubt that.

He turned off the light in his room and then in the darkness made out all of the objects he had just seen in the light. This process would allow his eyes to adjust to the darkness outside his door. As he walked down the hallway in his bare feet, he imagined he was invisible. During the three months he had lived in the house, he had made a mental note of where every squeaky or creaky floorboard was. He didn't remember when, why, or how, he just did, and his movements were stealthy because of it. *Is this what I look like when I'm sleepwalking, catlike in my movements? I am the silent soldier with two S's on my chest.* He smiled as he stopped in front of Miss Tracey's door.

One thought led to another, and something suddenly came to him. It wasn't the lock on his door that gave him his newfound privacy in his bedroom, but him standing up for himself—*well, standing up for Meri*. He looked back on that day four weeks ago when Miss Tracey tried to take Meri's phone by force during Meri's mythical call to the nonexistent Haven. He recalled those three words he used to make Miss Tracey stand down. *Let ... her ... go.* The whole scene almost made him laugh out loud.

As he walked into the bathroom and closed the door, he was careful not to disturb the silence. All the windows were closed in the house on this chilly October morning, effectively muting the familiar sounds outside to which he'd grown accustomed. He resisted turning on the light and relied instead on the sparse light that shone in through the bathroom window and on his night vision.

As he gazed in the mirror, he could just make out the main features of his face. The hairs on his chin seemed not to have grown a lick and were nonexistent in the scant light. He could see that the hair on his head had grown a little more, and it occurred to him that Miss Tracey had not mentioned a haircut—*a good thing, this standing up for yourself.* He wondered how else his life could be changed just by the mere act of speaking up when the situation called for it.

Life was good. Everything was fine, but something was missing. He wondered if he put himself out there and spoke up more often, could life be better? He wasn't having any fun, and he was getting restless. The last time he could remember anything exciting happening was that first day of school with Ham.

The images flashed through his mind: how Gruff held the knife against Naz's throat and pierced the skin, and how well Ham fought but ultimately went down with a knife wound to the stomach. But he was relieved he hadn't seen those boys since they came into MeeChi's the end of that first week, and he was fairly confident they wouldn't recognize him now, even if they did see him again. *Imagine me, in a gang. Why in the world would they want me anyway? They must've thought I was somebody else. They must've thought I was the biggest coward ... the way I just stood there ... and did nothing. But even after that, they still came for me at MeeChi's. I'm just glad it's over.* He thought about splashing water on his face, but again, he didn't want to disturb the perfect silence.

One thought connected to another, and when he had finished in the bathroom, he continued down the hallway thinking about Ham. Naz was glad Ham was OK, but he hadn't been looking forward to him coming to school for some reason, and his return more than justified Naz's apprehension. Since Ham's return to school the week before, he and Naz hadn't talked. Naz only had one class with Ham, and that happened to be Coach Fears' last hour health class.

He had overheard someone at lunch say Fears always made sure his basketball players ended up in his last hour class. That way he could make sure they were keeping their grades up and staying out of trouble. Naz wondered how he ended up landing in Fears' class. Then came the stares that coincided with the return of Ham—stares that signaled something had been said about what Naz had or hadn't done on that first day of school when he and Ham faced off with Gruff and Mohawk—*well Ham faced off*—that maybe he was a coward. What kids said about Naz didn't bother him, or at least it hadn't in the past. But something was changing inside of him. He didn't quite understand it and wasn't sure he liked it.

In his mind he, was accomplishing his goal as he continued on to Meri's room. He was changing his mindset, and now as he arrived at Meri's room, he placed his fingertips on the door, closed his eyes, and turned his head to listen. He wasn't sure if he could actually hear it, or if it was just in his imagination, but it was almost clear to him. Her phone was on, tuned to her favorite station, the oldies but goodies—*just like momma.* He shook his head to clear the thoughts that triggered the nightmare. He didn't know how she did it, but she could sleep with music playing all night. She had slept that way for over two years now, *ever since ...* Listening more carefully, Naz realized it wasn't her phone he could hear, but Meri humming or maybe singing, barely audible:

*"You may not understand me,*
*But I know these words you'll hear.*
*You'll never have to worry.*
*You'll never have to fear.*
*No way*
*I want to tell you this*
*Just before you fall off to sleep."*

It was a song, a lullaby their mother used to sing to Meri, but it was even more familiar to him than that. *Not again*—his mind returning to the nightmare.

As he made his way back to his room, he wondered if she were awake and thinking about her test in the morning. Was she nervous, or did she even care? He had promised to take her to the festival downtown after the test if she did her very best. They hadn't gone in over two years. *But how will I know if she did her best? Dr. Gwen won't know how she did until Monday.* But he had a feeling she would do her best because she always did her best. Meri wasn't as tied to Higginbotham or her friends there as much as she was to the Exclave itself. She had been to as many different schools as he had, in as many different years, so she hadn't put down any permanent roots either.

As he got back in bed, he decided the easiest way to avoid the nightmare would be to stay up the rest of the night. It was only a few hours before he would get up anyway. They needed to get an early start. The test was scheduled for nine o'clock in the morning. They would have to take the Helix: an automated, winding, elevated train that connected many parts of the Exclave to the suburbs and downtown. It would be an hour-and-a-half ride to International Academy. They had both been on the train a few times before with their mother, but never to the suburbs. His eyelids slowly grew heavy as he thought about how he and Meri had taken the Helix downtown to the festival with their mother. *Yesterday would've been Momma's birthday. We always went to the festival on Momma's birthday.*

"She loved to go to the festival," he said as he drifted in and out of consciousness. "Momma loved to go to the festival," he mumbled. As he gave in to sleep, one thought linked to another, and he was back in the nightmare—and, of course, he didn't realize it.

# 22: NIGHTMARE

Hey, Ma," said Naz, as his mother came through the front door. "Are we still going to the festival today?"

Camille had only worked half the day so she could go to the festival. "Yes, but you need to hurry up, both you and your sister. I told you to be ready when I got home."

"I am ready." Naz took off his guitar and threw it on the sofa.

"You know how he feels about you leaving things lying around. Where's your sister?"

"How would I know? Am I my sister's keeper?"

"Yes ... you *are*," she said pointedly "When I'm not here, you *are* your sister's keeper ... and you need to stop trying to quote the Bible ... or whatever you think you heard in Sunday School, you little heathen." She laughed.

Naz laughed as he grabbed his guitar and ran up the stairs.

"Hey, Ma!" called Meri as she passed Naz on her way down the stairs. "We still goin'?" She ran and gave her mother a leaping hug.

"My goodness, Meri. Of course ... I guess I don't have to ask if you're ready ... dressed like a little tomboy. We're gonna have to get you some pinks and some yellows and some—"

"I won't wear 'em!"

"I know you won't, but it's a nice thought."

Camille's expression changed as she heard a familiar sound. She moved to look out the front window. Her greatest fear was realized. It was her husband, Bearn, home from work early. She had promised him she wouldn't go to the festival anymore, but she couldn't stay away. She figured she could take a half-day off here or there, and no one would know. She didn't think she had to worry about Naz or Meri telling Bearn because they knew the ramifications all too well.

"Go upstairs with your brother."

"But, Ma—"

"Now! What did I tell you about talking so much, Meri? Now go!" She tried to appear calm, but the urgency in her voice gave her desperation away.

Meri ran up the stairs to find Naz looking out the window in his room.

"What is he doing here?" Naz asked. "He never gets off early."

Meri joined him at the window. "And he doesn't look happy either. Why is he just sitting there?" she asked.

"Because he's thinking."

"Thinking about what?"

"It doesn't matter. When he gets done, it's not gonna be anything nice. He must've found out we're going to the festival."

"So what? What's the big deal about going to the festival? He can go with us."

"No, he can't!"

"Why not?"

"I don't know, but he can't!" And then it came to him. He looked at Meri suspiciously. "You told him."

"He already knew. He called home an hour ago and asked what time we were leaving."

"He didn't know, Meri. He tricked you. I told you; you can't trust him."

"He's my dad."

"I know but ... I thought I told you not to answer the phone anyway."

"I kept telling you the phone was ringing, but you were playing that stupid guitar with your headphones on, and I tried—"

"Wait!" He put his hand up to stop her from talking. "He's getting out."

A native of the Exclave with no hope of parole, Bearn Slaughter was by any measure a giant of a man. He easily stood six-foot-six and tipped the scales at a whopping three-hundred-plus pounds. He had thick, wavy, jet-black hair that he always wore in a single braid down his back. Bearn had failed at almost everything he tried but was a master manipulator, and Naz had heard on the streets that this skill often got him in or back in whatever game he had set his sights on. Word had it that he used this skill of manipulation to ensnare Camille during a time of uncertainty. In Naz's opinion, Bearn was a bully and a fiend, and he wondered what his mother ever saw in him. *Could my father have been anything like "him?"* His physical stature was matched only by his temper, which was in full force today as he stumbled his way up the porch stairs and into the Slaughter house.

"Maybe we should call somebody," said Meri.

"Who? Momma has nobody else ... but us."

"The police."

"Like the last two times? They never came anyway," he said, shaking his head.

"Well, we've got to do something!"

"Shhh ...."

The door opened and shut. They could hear Camille say, "*Hey, honey,*" and that was all. There was a crack that resembled the sound of a lone firecracker on the Fourth of July. Meri immediately bolted down the stairs.

"Meri!" Naz called. He swore and then mumbled to himself, "I am my sister's keeper," as he shot down the stairs after her.

"Daddy!" Meri screamed as she flew down the stairs.

"I told you not to call me that!" Bearn yelled as he turned to put his huge finger in Meri's face.

"Get your hand out of her face!" Camille shouted. She was holding the side of her face where Bearn had just struck her.

Bearn was holding Camille's wrist, and in swift retaliation for her command, he hit her again with his closed hand on the side of her head, this time sending her crashing to the floor like a rag doll. Knowing Camille would run, he never let go of her wrist.

Meri screamed and covered her ears.

"Shut up, brat!" shouted Bearn at Meri, but she kept screaming.

"Let her go!" pleaded Naz.

Bearn ignored Naz as if he wasn't in the room.

"Let her go, Bearn!" Naz shouted again, as Meri kept screaming and crying.

With blood streaming down the side of her head, Camille had already made one attempt to get up, but dazed, she fell back to the floor, half dangling as Bearn maintained his vise-like grip around her wrist. Meri continued to scream and cry frantically.

"I told you to shut up!" said Bearn as he made a motion to hit Meri with his free hand.

"Leave her alone!" Naz implored.

"And I told you not to go there anymore, didn't I? You're not going anywhere ... again ... ever," Bearn threatened Camille.

*What does that mean?* Naz thought.

"I'll go anywhere I want!" Camille managed to shout back in anger. She was still dazed and trying to get to her feet.

Naz saw the look on Bearn's face, and he knew his mother was about to die if he didn't help her. He looked for something—anything—to bring Bearn down, but nothing was lying around. His guitar would've made a nice weapon going upside Bearn's head, but he didn't have time to retrieve it. He had to think fast. When Bearn reared back to hit Camille again, Naz ran into Bearn with everything he had. He knocked the giant back and managed to free his mother.

"Run, Ma!" Naz screamed.

Meri stopped screaming and ran over to Camille.

"Come on, Ma. Get up," she said, helping Camille to her feet.

Naz stood facing Bearn.

"Oh, I've been waiting for this. There's nothing special about you." Bearn sneered at Naz with a smile.

Naz looked puzzled, and Bearn rounded on him in a second. Naz made Bearn miss twice, but his mistake came when he tried to block Bearn's punch. He hit Naz on the side of the jaw with a glancing blow that sent him flying back and up into the air. Naz landed on his back and immediately jumped to his feet only to fall back down again. He lay there with his eyes closed not quite sure where he was. When he opened his eyes, the world looked slightly fractured, and he saw two of everything. He closed his eyes and shook his head, but when he opened them again nothing had changed, so he closed them once again.

But then finally, someone was there to help them. Naz couldn't see them, but he could hear them—*or was it just one person?* It didn't matter. It was a man's voice, a voice he wasn't sure he recognized, but the man arrived just in time.

"*What are you doing? I'll kill you!*" the voice said.

Relieved, Naz opened his eyes to his fractured world again to see his mother on Bearn's back. She hit him relentlessly on his shoulders, neck, and back of the head, all while screaming words Naz had never heard her say before. Meri was screaming again, too.

*But where's the man? Why isn't he helping?*

"*I'll kill you!*" the voice said again.

*Well, get on with it,* Naz thought.

"*Somebody help, somebody help,*" the voice kept saying.

Naz realized, just as he could feel himself losing consciousness that no one was there to help him or Meri. No one was there to save his mother. Just before his eyes closed, he saw his mother flying through the air, and he heard a crash and glass breaking. He loved his mother a lot but hated Bearn even more, and now he wanted him dead. What would he and Meri do without their mother? He imagined himself as a giant, even bigger than Bearn. He put his huge hands around Bearn's pitiful neck, and with all the love, anger, and fear he could muster, he squeezed the life out of Bearn. There was a loud thud and then Naz was awake again.

He opened his eyes to find Meri sitting on the steps. He walked over to her, fear focusing his eyes only on her, afraid to look around. He touched the side of his head. His face was numb and horribly swollen. He was thinking his jaw at the very least must be broken, and he could hear a constant ringing in his ear. Meri's eyes were red, but there were no more tears. When he tried to speak, the pain was unbearable.

With no emotion, Meri gave an almost imperceptible nod, directing him to turn around. Bearn lay there motionless on his back, his head to the side. He had one hand around his neck and white foam coming from his mouth. Unmoved by this scene, Naz turned slowly to see first his mother's legs, then the rest of her in a bed of blood and glass. Bearn had thrown her through the dining room table.

"Ma!" Naz gave a strangled yell, as he sat up and saw Meri sitting at the foot of his bed.

# 23: HAPPY BIRTHDAY MA′

What are you doing?" Naz asked, sitting up disoriented. "How'd you get in here?"

"It wasn't locked," said Meri, looking at his bedroom door.

"I forgot to lock it."

"Momma?"

Naz nodded, looking at the clock on his nightstand. "Why are you up anyway? You should be asleep. You worried about the test?"

"No." She shook her head.

"Is it Momma?"

"Uh-huh." She nodded in camaraderie.

"So, what do you wanna do?"

She smiled, jumped off the bed and then returned a second later from under his bed with his chess set.

"Now?" he asked.

"We have time," she said, looking at his clock. "Why is this still under your bed anyway?"

"I was hoping that if I left it there, you would forget about it."

"Not likely," she said, smiling deviously.

"I should've never taught you how to play. I really don't feel like playing."

"I think you're just scared."

"Your little mind games don't work on me. You'll have to do better than that if you wanna get me to play." He paused in shallow thought for a few seconds and then nodded his head and continued. "Actually, I could work off some stress. Maybe I will beat up on you again."

"You're gonna lose, 'cause you're already rattled from your little nightmare, but not yet, we have to sing 'Happy Birthday' first."

"We what?" he asked, baffled.

"'Happy Birthday.' Today would've been Momma's birthday and—"

"Yesterday would've been Momma's birthday."

"Look," she said, pointing to the window. "The sun hasn't come up yet, so as far as I'm concerned, it's not a new day. Anyway, every year we go through this and never say anything about it. You end up having nightmares, and I can't sleep."

"And you think this will help?"

"I think if we don't talk about it, it'll just keep building up. We need to purge."

"Purge? You read too much."

"You don't read enough."

"Says who?" He put his head down again for a moment and then looked up and conceded. "OK, I'll make a deal with you. We get to take turns asking each other questions—any questions we want—and the other one has to answer, or the deal's off and no birthday song."

"How many questions?"

"As many as it takes until we're both satisfied."

"Only if I get to go first," Meri said excitedly.

"So let it be written. So let it be done."

"And when we're *done*, we sing."

"I guess."

"No. We have to shake on it. Deal," she said.

They shook hands the old-fashioned way.

## 24: REVELATIONS

Meri set up the chess set placing the white pieces on her side, made her first move and then said, "Tell me about your nightmare."

"That's not a question, and this is gonna be a short game if that's your best move," said Naz.

"OK, what did you dream about?"

"That's a wasted question. You know what I dreamed about. It's always the same. Although, I am different in the dream now."

"How?"

He made his first move and then replied, "I'm older, like I am now, and everyone else is the same. But it doesn't make a difference. She still dies."

"She was murdered. He killed her."

"The coroner said both causes of death were accidents. He was your dad. Do you really think he meant to kill her? It's your move by the way." Naz loved his mother but blamed her for something he could not explain. It was just a feeling. If nothing else, he resented her for the years he couldn't remember and for her absence from them.

"I know," she said, frustrated. "And he wasn't my dad. I don't have a dad. And how can you say that? She was your mother, too. You didn't see what I saw. Your eyes were closed."

"Now we're getting somewhere. Tell me what you saw, Meri. I mean, what did you see that day? Tell me everything."

She moved one of her chess pieces and then swallowed hard. "You sure you wanna know?"

He nodded, countering her move immediately.

Meri stared at the board and took a deep breath. "After he hit you, Momma jumped on his back and started hitting him on his shoulders and head." Meri closed her eyes. "He reached up, grabbed her by the arms, and flung her over his head onto the dining room table."

Naz knew all of this from what she had told the police, but he also knew there was more she hadn't told the police, something she kept from them and everyone else.

"What else, Meri? Do you remember what happened after I passed out?"

"Like it was yesterday. And ... you never passed out," she said, making her next move.

"Slow down and concentrate. You're gonna make a careless mistake in a minute."

"I know what I'm doing. Anyway, you were sitting there with your eyes closed, but you weren't unconscious. What were you doing?"

"It was the first time I heard the voices ... well, voice. I thought that somebody had come to help. That's when I think I passed out," he said, sliding one of his pieces across the board.

"After he threw Momma, he turned toward me. I looked at you just sitting there with your eyes closed, and I knew he would kill me next and then you. That's when I cried. I cried every tear I had, and I prayed the way Momma taught me. Then, something happened. 'He' grabbed his throat, and for a long time he tried to cough or talk or something, but nothing came out. Then, he fell flat on his back and never moved again. I wiped my eyes, and that's when you got up and walked over to me."

Naz was silent for a while as he pondered her words.

She picked up one of her white pieces and put it in the place of one of his black pieces. Removing his black piece from the board, she added, "And it wasn't the first time I saw you do that, either."

"Do what? What do you mean? What did I do?"

"It's my turn."

"Wait, hold up ..."

"No, it's my turn!"

Naz nodded his head as he relented.

"What do you remember about your dad?" she asked.

"That's not fair. We're talkin' about Momma."

"So what? Our deal wasn't limited to Momma. You said we could ask whatever we wanted. You came up with the rules."

"But—"

"But nothin'."

He nodded again, studied the chessboard for a moment and then jumped up to grab his guitar. He sat back on the bed and made his move. "I haven't played this in a long time," he said, tuning his guitar.

"You're stalling."

"OK, I don't remember ... anything ... maybe shadows ... and emotions, but not him, not how he looked or sounded. Sometimes I hear those oldies when you're listening to the radio, and I can remember all the words. And while the music is playing, I can see rooms and can even make out furniture. I can even remember lines to movies that I can't remember ever watching. That happens all the time."

"Trust me. I know," she said sarcastically.

"When I'm outside sometimes, and I smell certain plants or flowers, I get excited and content at the same time, because I imagine parks, beautiful parks that you could never find in the Exclave, and I know that I've been there before. But there are never people, never my dad in those places. It's like a puzzle of my life, but some of the pieces are missing. It's hard to figure out what goes where, and it gets frustrating.

"So now when those feelings come, I do my best to ignore them. I think that's why Dr. Gwen calls them repressed memories, a type of retrograde amnesia because I consciously reject the memories." He resisted getting frustrated because talking to Meri like this had a calming effect on him. He could never talk this openly and freely with anyone else, not even Dr. Gwen.

"Do you remember the car accident?" she asked, advancing a harmless pawn.

"Not at all, I only know what they told me, that I was thrown from the car and my dad wasn't and that he likely died on impact. I only remember waking up in a hospital to a stranger that said she was my mother."

"Do you know what he looked like? Do you have any pictures?"

"I asked Momma if I could see a picture when we got home from the hospital, but she said she didn't have any ... no surprise there. 'He' wouldn't even let her mention his name."

"And his name was Cory?"

"Yep, Cory Andersen, and that's all I know about him," he said, moving one of his pieces and taking one of hers in the process. He stuck his tongue out at her. "Now, how many questions was that? Time to pay up with some answers of your own. When was the last time you cried ... about anything?"

"The last time you saw me cry ... that day ... when he killed her and you ..."

"And I what?"

"And you saved me," she said, countering his move and taking another one of his pieces.

"What do you mean? How did I save you?"

She decided not to answer.

Not sure if he wanted to hear the answer, Naz continued. "And why don't you cry anymore? Everybody has to cry. It's natural," he said, moving his knight out of harm's way and into striking position.

"I know. But that day, when I cried and cried and cried, I ... I cried because it was my fault. It was my fault that he found out. It was my fault that he came home that day and ..." her voice trembled. She swallowed hard. "It was my fault that he killed her."

"Don't you ever say that again. You had nothing to do with it. It was him, and only him. It was bound to happen eventually regardless of what you did because he was a bad man, and Momma didn't have sense enough to leave him."

"It *was* my fault."

"Stop it!" Naz's temper rose.

"I prayed, and I promised God that if He delivered me and my brother that day, I would never cry again. Who would've known that He had already answered my prayer the year before by sending me you?" she said, making an aggressive move on his queen.

"What are you talking about?"

"What else do you know about your father?"

"Just that, like Momma, he was some kind of teacher and that he gave me a stupid name.

"A stupid name?" she laughed. "Why do you hate your name so much?"

"Because it's stupid. You know it's stupid. It's not even a name. It's what you get when you cross a computer with a deity," he said laughing.

"You're silly, but I still like your name," she said, laughing along with him.

"Then it's yours; you can have it," he said, countering her aggressive move. "Did you know you had a brother before I came here three years ago?"

"No, but that first day they brought you home, I knew I had seen you at least two other times before."

"When?" he asked curiously, his eyes opening wide.

"Well," she said, moving another one of her pieces. "When I was about four ... or five, I would go shopping with Momma. We would go to different stores and shop all day long for this and that." She had to pause. Reminiscing about the good old days with her mother caused her to become misty-eyed, and she was about to renege on her promise to God. She cleared her throat and continued. "Twice we went on a long ride to the suburbs, and Momma stopped at this beautiful park that was like nothing I had ever seen before. The grass was like thick, green carpet, and there was no trash anywhere. The playscapes were so colorful. It was like candy: lollipops and licorice."

Naz closed his eyes as she continued.

"There were different kinds of slides and swings, curvy slides, straight slides, and tunnel slides, and swings made out of tires. I liked the tire swings the best, because they reminded me of home, only cleaner, and there was nothing dangerous about these tires like ours, no nails sticking out or anything. The ground was soft and colorful, or made of wood chips that smelled like ... I don't know, outdoor freshie." She laughed.

"Outdoor freshie? What is that?" he said, laughing as he opened his eyes.

"I don't know, but it's the only way I can describe it."

"I can see it, too," he said, closing his eyes again.

"It's your move," she snapped at him.

He jumped, and his eyes sprang open again. "I know. I'll get to it. You shouldn't be in such a hurry to lose. Tell me more about the park," he said, moving one of his chess pieces without thinking about it. He closed his eyes again. He knew she was studying the chessboard carefully, meaning to take advantage of what she thought was a careless move on his part. *She'll probably go in for the kill on her very next move*—but he didn't care. His mind was no longer on the game. It was in the park. He was in the park.

"Then, there was my most favorite thing of all, the monkey bars," she continued. "That's when I saw you for the first time. You were on the very top of the monkey bars, and your hair was a lot longer than it is now, and wilder."

Naz stopped playing his guitar and began to twist his hair.

She continued as if she were telling the greatest story ever told. "Your arms were straight up over your head, but you weren't hanging from the highest bar, you were in a handstand on the top of it. You were perfectly still. I don't think anyone noticed, but me. I turned my head upside down, and it was like you were holding the whole world, monkey bars and all, over your head. I pointed and said, 'Look!' All the other kids started looking, pointing, and cheering you on. Then, you swung down around another bar, back into the air, did some kind of flip and then landed with both feet on the ground. Everybody started clapping and ran over to you. We were all asking you questions, but you wouldn't say anything. You just looked at everyone and smiled. I looked over and saw Momma sitting on a bench clapping, too, with the biggest smile. I never saw her smile like that before.

"We came back a couple of months later," she continued. "I don't know if I was more interested in seeing that beautiful park again or seeing the amazing kid that could fly on the monkey bars. We must've stayed there for hours waiting. Momma never said it, but I got the feeling she was waiting for you, too. It was getting late, and Daddy ... I mean, 'he' would've had a fit if we came home too late. I think we were just about to leave when two boys got into a shoving match. Well, it really wasn't a match. One boy was bullying another one who was half his size. When I turned to leave, Momma got up and was walking away with a man I had never seen before.

"That's when I heard a boy shout, 'Leave him alone.' I turned back around to see it was you who said it. The bully stopped, looked up and then you said, 'Why don't you pick on somebody your own size?' This sounded strange to me because you were no bigger than the boy he was picking on. The bully said, 'Why don't you make me, runt?' Then, you went off. You said something about him being a bed wetter, sleeping with his light on, failing the fourth grade, and some other stuff, too, but you sounded like a grown-up. Everybody started laughing."

"Weren't there any grown-ups around?"

"Yeah, but we were all laughing, so I guess they thought we were just playing ... having fun. That's when the bully got really mad and came charging at you. You just moved out of the way and stuck your foot out, and he went flying past you and landed under the swings in the wood chips. Everybody really started laughing then. When he came at you the second time, he tried to hit you in the head twice, but you ducked both times, and he missed. Then, you dropped down and did something with your leg like it was a broom. The bully flew straight into the air and landed on his butt.

"By this time, everybody went crazy. When the bully looked up and saw the boy he was bullying holding his side laughing, he got up, put him in some kind of headlock and started choking him. I heard you yell 'let him go.' What happened next, happened fast. Everybody started screaming, and I could see Momma and the man running toward the crowd. Through the crowd of kids, I could see you standing with your arms out and your eyes closed, and the bully was on the ground shaking. The next thing I knew Momma had grabbed me by my wrist, and we were running to the car. While we were driving away, I could hear the sound of sirens getting louder. Then I saw an ambulance pass us. I looked back to see it turning into the park.

"When you came home from the hospital a few months ... maybe a year or so later ... you were a little taller and your hair was gone, but I knew it was—"

PART THREE
**DISSOLUTION**

## IN THE PAST...

**B**efore the audience can adjust to the darkness, Cory engages the projector. On the screen is shown a random sample of forty preschool-aged children divided into two groups of twenty. The children are seen watching a series of amusing animated short films of children slightly older than themselves gathering information and making decisions about various stimuli without the traditional use of their five senses. The children in the films are using a combination of their five senses in nontraditional ways, along with a sixth sense, simply referred to as mind.

In the films, a little girl has the ability—with uncanny accuracy—to predict and/or influence what a person will do, given a specific set of choices, by just having physical contact with that person. One boy outperforms a lie detector machine by simply making eye contact with the subject in question. Two children celebrate their achievement when they can solve a complex mathematical problem together simply by mutual focus, meditation, and concentration.

Group A, the control group, is told that they are simply watching a cartoon meant for their enjoyment before they embark on a yearlong adventure learning camp. Group B, the experimental group, is told explicitly that the events depicted in the animated short films are true and that through the yearlong adventure learning camp they will acquire the same abilities exhibited by the cartoon characters in the films.

The children in the study are then shown participating in various activities of the yearlong learning camp. In the film, the children traverse random and ever-changing obstacle courses daily by using only their senses of hearing, touch, and smell. They are encouraged to use their imagination to see things that are not there and explain how those things affect the outcome of certain events. The children participate in daily individual and small group prayer, meditation, and visualization exercises for the purpose of solving specific problems related to adventure games played at the camp.

When the film is over, the screen and stage go dark simultaneously, and the house lights come on to reveal Cory with a handheld microphone in the middle aisle of the auditorium, as he addresses the audience around him.

"'Necessity ... is the mother of invention' is a saying attributed to no one, but applicable to all," says Cory. "At some point or another in all of our lives, we change because we must. Our situation dictates ... no, demands it. History is replete with examples of people not having or losing one or more of their five senses leading to an enhancement of their remaining ones. A visually impaired person's senses of hearing, smell, touch, and even taste often far surpass those senses in a person with no visual impairment. What if we, by intention, develop our own five senses the way these impaired people develop their remaining ones, and then enhance those five senses with a sixth sense—mind, which connects them all?" asks Cory, pointing to his own head.

Cory continues as he paces up and down the aisle. "One of the biggest myths that still persists is that we only use ten percent of our brains. Better than ninety percent of the graduate students that come to me still believe this. It has never made sense to me. But I too wanted to believe so badly that there was more up here," says Cory as he points to his head again, "that was untapped. I mean come on, if we were only using ten percent of our brains, imagine what we could do if we were to triple that output ... or just double it. When I learned the truth—that we use all of our brains—I remember saying to myself, 'Well that sucks!'"

The audience laughs.

"But then it occurred to me that even though we may use all of our brains, we don't nearly use it to its fullest potential. It's akin to lifting a pencil over our heads," says Cory, as he lifts his arm over his head, back behind his neck and shoulders and then back up to reveal a pencil. "I'm using my whole arm ... or am I?" He reaches back down behind his neck and shoulders and then up again to reveal a fifteen-pound dumbbell instead of the pencil.

The audience murmurs.

"Ah ... that's more like it. Now I'm using my whole arm ... and then some, I believe," he says as he playfully struggles to put the dumbbell down beside him and then rubs his shoulder.

Some in the audience laugh, but some are beginning to lose patience.

"No, we don't nearly use our minds to their fullest potential," says Cory. "We only apply them to the obvious ... the outside, what we can see, touch, taste, hear, and smell. I tell you there is more."

"Noted philosopher, Robert Darryl Glenn wrote, 'It is not as much about faith in the unseen, as it is belief in the possibilities within.' Indeed, when it comes to our own capabilities and limitations, belief liberates while doubt incarcerates."

The uneasy audience begins to murmur again.

One amused gentleman, a reporter who is seated near Cory, raises his hand. Cory moves to him and hands him the microphone.

"Yes, sir?" asks Cory.

"Now, are we talking about psychic powers, Dr. Andersen ... I mean, Mr. Anders?" asks the reporter mockingly.

There is sparse laughter throughout the auditorium.

"Psychic powers?" asks Cory, keeping his composure. "Those are your words. What you see here today is simply heightened application of our five senses and the mind. But you tell me," says Cory dramatically as he abruptly points to the stage.

With Cory's movements, the house lights go off, and the stage lights come on to reveal a small girl standing next to a bicycle with training wheels. The podium and screen are gone and behind her is what appears to be an obstacle course with artificial bushes, tree stumps, miniature park benches, signs, and a red plastic fire hydrant. Cory asks the reporter to join him on stage.

After he and the reporter take the stage, Cory introduces the girl as Darla to the audience and blindfolds her. He asks the reporter to rearrange the course to his liking making sure to leave a path wide enough for the bicycle to navigate. As the reporter finishes rearranging the course, he accidentally knocks over one of the bushes.

"Never can trust those eyes, can ya?" says Cory sarcastically to the audience, at the expense of the reporter's clumsiness and to make a point of his own.

The audience laughs.

"Now that we know that Darla can't have memorized the course, there's just one more thing," says Cory as he escorts the reporter back off of the stage. "Since there is no way to convince all of you that she actually cannot see through the blindfold, how about we all go blind." He snaps his fingers, and the auditorium goes completely dark.

# 25: CHECKMATE

## PRESENT DAY...

Stop it!" he said in a muffled yell, startling her. "I know you have a queen-sized imagination, but enough is enough!"

"But Naz—"

"I said, enough!" He looked at the chessboard with renewed concentration. Five seconds later he made a confident move.

She shrugged her shoulders and made a confident move of her own. "Check," she said.

"Impressive. Most impressive, but you are not a Jedi yet." It was his best Darth Vader imitation.

"You need to quit with the impressions."

He made a move that freed his king from the grips of her knight. She countered, this time challenging his king with a vulnerable rook. But in her overzealousness, she grew careless, leaving her king unguarded.

"Check," she said, less confident than before.

"The Firecracker from Higginbotham strikes back with a bold move," Naz commented as if it were some televised sporting event.

"Would you shut up and just play."

"Oh ... too much pressure, huh?" Naz said capturing her rook and freeing his king once more.

"Just play!"

"But no, could it be the Nazarite from Lincoln who deals the final death blow?" On his very next move, he swooped down on her king with his queen and trapped the monarch from all sides. "Checkmate!" he said triumphantly, taunting her.

In one aggressive motion, she cleared the board with her arm, sending all of the wooden chess pieces scattering on the hardwood floor beneath them.

Surprised, Naz stood up and ordered, "Pick 'em up!"

She stood up angrily with her arms folded, still as a statue. "But I did everything right. My moves were right. I should've won."

"Pick them up now."

They stood and stared at each other for almost a minute. Finally, Meri's angry stare transformed into a smile, and the two began to laugh quietly.

"Your moves were right ... if your moves were right, you would've won," said Naz.

"You told me always to think three moves ahead, and that's what I did."

"But not just with one piece, Meri, all the pieces, including and especially your opponent's pieces."

"That's impossible. How am I supposed to know what move you're gonna make next?"

"You have to anticipate ... or guess."

"I know what anticipate means."

"Well, anticipate. You have to look down over the board, see all the pieces and possibilities, and make your moves based on what you know your opponent will likely do next. You have to know what to protect and what not to protect and when and where to sacrifice something. And yes, you have to sacrifice something to win. It might even be your queen."

"So, look down on the board," she said, concentrating intently, "and see all the pieces, huh ... kinda like how God looks down and sees all of us?"

"Huh? What? No, Meri, not like God. It's not always about God. God had nothing to do with you winning or losing the game."

"Momma said that God has something to do with everything."

"Where was God that day, Meri?"

She put her head down and didn't answer.

"What did God have to do with Momma being thrown through that table?" he asked.

"Momma said that God works—"

"In mysterious ways," Naz interrupted, finishing her sentence. "I know, and that we shouldn't question His infinite wisdom ... part of some divine plan ... blah blah blah and yada yada yada. I will always question what happened to Momma and injustice in any form, and I don't like His mysterious ways. When something good happens, it's always all glory to God, then when something bad happens, it's always our wretched souls or the devil at work, and I'm not buying it."

"Don't you believe in God?"

He paused for a moment. "I don't know, at least not the way I've been taught for sure. It just doesn't make sense."

"That's why you got kicked out of Sunday School."

"Clearly."

"Then, why do you keep that out?" she said pointing to the Bible on his nightstand.

"It was the only thing Miss Tracey let me keep out before, so why put it away now? I think she was too afraid to tell me to put it away. I mean ... it is a Bible after all. Who in their right mind would tell you to put a Bible up and risk the wrath of ... well, fire and brimstone?" he said sarcastically.

"How did you learn how to play chess this well anyway?"

"I don't know. I'm guessing my dad taught me."

"How does that work?"

"What do you mean?"

"When did you find out you could play?"

"You know the Chess Master at the festival ... the one with all the tables?"

"Yeah."

"The last time we were at the festival with Momma, I wandered off to the tables and just started playing. I guess you could say, I knew without knowing."

"That's weird. Did you win?"

"When Momma noticed me over there, she pulled me away, and I never got a chance to finish the game."

"Have you ever lost?"

"Not that I can remember."

"Wow, how come you don't play for Lincoln?"

"Because it's boring. It's too easy."

"So, what else do you think you know ... I mean, without knowing?" She asked what he was already thinking, and he wasn't paying attention to her question.

He looked at the clock. "It's time."

"But Naz—"

"Go!" He pointed to his door. "Go get ready."

"Not until you pay up."

He looked at her confused. She started singing "Happy Birthday," and he begrudgingly sang along with her.

# 26: THE HELIX

It was hard for Naz to know what section or borough they were traveling through as he looked out of the window and down from the automated, high-speed, winding train. They had been out of Marshal Park for over twenty minutes now, but there was no doubt in his mind he was still in the Exclave—*Aquinas Grove*. The buildings were the same. The houses were the same. It was as if they were going in circles, and with the never-ending turns of the Helix, he wasn't so sure they weren't. It was only the different streets, market names, and strange faces that assured him of their forward progress.

And there it was: the monstrosity. Major General, one of the Mega Chain superstores was just below him. He had been there once with his mother and remembered how amazing it was. *They have everything*. In fact, he couldn't think of anything they didn't have. He never told Mr. Tesla he had been to Major General before. Naz wasn't sure how he would react, with him despising the store so. As the train sped by, he noticed several men on scaffolds as they tried to remove graffiti that had likely gone up the night before.

Naz looked over at Meri who was fast asleep with her head on his shoulder. She had fallen asleep even before the train left the station, and now the hum and vibration of the Helix made his eyelids heavy as well. He had learned a lot about Meri that morning and even more about himself—things that excited him, things that scared him, and things that he wasn't prepared to believe. Then from nowhere, sleep took him like a hammer blow, and he was out like a light.

IN WHAT SEEMED to him like seconds later, his eyes popped open in surprise as Meri nudged him with her elbow.

"Look," she said, pointing out the window.

They were in the Exclave no more, and there were trees as far as the eye could see.

Naz rubbed his eyes and took in the gorgeous, dense green forest that the train was now weaving through. "What time is it?" he asked concerned.

Meri was too caught up in the spectacle to hear his question. She had been to the suburbs twice before with their mother, but never on the train where she was so high up and so close. Naz pulled out his phone to check the time. He had been asleep for almost an hour, which meant they would be at International Academy soon.

"Are you ready?" he asked.

She didn't answer.

"Meri!"

"How can you think about that stupid test when you look out there and see all of that?" She pointed out the window to the wall of trees.

"They're just trees ... and I knew you heard me. You know, we do have trees at home."

"Not like those."

"We're almost there. You need to get ready."

"And how do you suppose I do that?"

"I don't know. Think smart thoughts or something."

The train rolled into a clearing to reveal a row of buildings with brilliant architecture encircling a lavish park, much like what Meri had described earlier that morning. Naz immediately looked at Meri. She shook her head. A little further along there were more majestic trees and a series of small lakes, followed by a stretch of elegant buildings, some seemingly made of all glass and some made of glass and smooth, shiny stone—*maybe marble.*

There were structures so breathtaking neither Naz nor Meri could remember seeing their equal other than on television or in the movies. They could not predict what would come next because no building was like the one that preceded it, and there was no rhyme, reason, or pattern to the landscape. The sun reflected off the buildings and lakes to add to the grandeur of it all. Then another park came into view that was even more magnificent than the first, and Naz again looked at Meri in hopeful anticipation. She again shook her head.

"Now tell me again. Why do you wanna live in the Exclave?" asked Naz.

"Because it's my home. Why can't our home look like that?" she asked pointing out the window again.

He thought about her question but didn't respond, assuming it was rhetorical in nature. The two watched in silence as the train finally began to slow.

## 27: THE BURBS

Before exiting the train, Naz took one last look at the map Dr. Gwen had given him. Then, he folded it and put it in his pocket for good. During the mile-long walk from the train station to International Academy, he didn't want to look lost or like they didn't belong, and in his mind, walking around reading a map would reveal just that. In the Exclave, walking around in a similar fashion was akin to bleeding in shark-infested waters, and it was only a matter of time before a predator would strike.

But here, it wasn't that way. There was calmness all about— still waters. It was an open area with spacious scenery, breathtaking houses, and well-manicured lawns. Naz felt calm in this setting, a calm he never knew at home. After a few blocks, they approached what appeared to be a strip of stores and other businesses. Because it was still early, most of these were closed, and there weren't many people out and about. Even so, you could still inside the shops and businesses through the massive glass walls, doors, and windows. And like the houses and buildings, they were all different.

In one store, there were racks and racks of fancy clothes, some sported by aerodynamic-looking mannequins. In another store, there were endless shoes in every aisle. In still another, there were rows and columns of glass bottles in different colors, shapes, and sizes—*some like the kind "he" always brought home*. And there were restaurants—a myriad of restaurants.

In the Exclave, it was either the Market Merchants for most things or the Mega Chains for everything else. And when they were closed, they were closed, locked down with no way to see inside. A flexible bulletproof metal door covered the only glass window of the markets when they were closed, and the Mega Chains had no windows to cover up.

When they reached the corner, Meri said in surprise, "Look," then took off in the direction she was pointing.

Naz, being used to her impulsiveness, didn't cry out but instead shook his head and followed her. He looked around only to discover this wasn't a strip at all, but a maze of stores, shops, restaurants, theaters, and other businesses.

By the time he caught up to her, she had found a hobby shop. In front of the shop was a life-sized chess set. In the shop window could be seen chess sets with pieces made of glass, stone, wood, metal, and other materials. There were computerized and electronic chess sets and even chess sets where the pieces were moving by themselves. There were also toys, model cars, boats, and planes, and a variety of train sets in motion, but Meri only had eyes for the chess sets.

"Well?" she asked.

"Well, what?" He was as impressed as Meri but was determined to arrive at International Academy on time.

"Let's play," she said deviously, as she tried to move one of the giant pawns of the chess set. It was as tall as she was, and she couldn't budge it.

"Good," he laughed. "Serves you right. Now who's stalling? Didn't you get enough of losing this morning?"

"Look!" She ran over and jumped on the back of one of the giant knights. "I'm Ron," she said in a passable English accent.

"No, that would be me. Now let's go. You're not gonna be late for this test, Meri."

She shrugged, as he grabbed her hand, and they went back in the direction from which they came. But, as he had feared, they were now turned around. He wasn't even sure if the map would help at this point. He tried to retrace their steps, but nothing looked the same.

Some of the restaurants were open, and one in particular with outside seating was serving breakfast. Naz and Meri walked by and were greeted with friendly nods, something unseen in the Exclave. Eye contact with strangers was a no-no in the Exclave, signaling disrespect, fear, or a show of intimidation, depending on the parties involved.

*If I don't find the way soon, the opportunity will be lost, and like Dr. Gwen said, there will be no second chance. I will have failed Meri.* He cast the thought out his mind, and at that very moment a couple walking their dog stopped them, asked if they were brother and sister and if they were lost. *Was it that obvious even without the map in my hand?* Naz nodded and told them where he and Meri were headed. The couple smiled and pointed them in the right direction. They thanked the couple and were off.

With no time to lose, once they were out of the maze, Naz told Meri to get on his back, and he ran. He wouldn't chance her being even one minute late. All the while he quizzed her on the words Dr. Gwen had given him that would help her on the test. With each word, she grew more and more irritated and impatient. But he didn't care. Then, he had a flash—a memory. Someone somewhere had treated him this same way before, the way he was now treating Meri.

"What does categorize mean?" he quizzed her.

"To place in a particular group or class," she rattled off, robotically.

"Use it in a sentence."

"I categorize these questions as useless because I already know this stuff."

Naz tutted. "State the meaning of the word, hypothesize."

"Are you serious?"

"Yes!"

"To put forth a hypothesis."

"Define hypothesis."

"An educated guess."

"Use summarize in a sentence."

"Really?"

"Really!" Naz could tell she was done.

She thought for a moment and then in her best Southern belle accent said, "Summarize ... Dis summer I's goin' to da festival wit ma big brutha."

Naz stopped dead in his tracks and put her down. "What?"

"Summarize ... Dis summer I's goin' to da festival wit ma big brutha," she repeated playfully.

He thought about it and started laughing. "You foolish. You shoulda just said so if you didn't wanna study."

"Do I have to spell it out?"

"Yup," he said, laughing as they approached International Academy.

# 28: INTERNATIONAL ACADEMY

When they arrived at International Academy, it wasn't at all what Naz had expected. There were no modern buildings made of glass, granite, or marble but a historic little village of sorts. It seemed to be completely surrounded by a tall wrought iron fence.

At the gates, cars pulled into a drive, and on each gate were the giant Old English style letters "I" and "A." The initials made Naz think of the raised crest on the envelope Dr. Gwen had given him, the envelope that contained Meri's letter. He and Meri got behind the last car and followed the line of cars up to a booth. Naz showed Meri's letter to the attendant and was given a map directing him to the building where Meri would take the test.

They arrived at the building with a little time to spare. Many children, big and small, made their way inside. Some parents were apparently giving last minute encouragement. Naz knew from the instructions in the letter he would not be allowed to enter the building with her, so he bent down where he stood and took out one of his shoestrings.

"What are you doing?" Meri asked.

"I wanna give you something."

"A dirty shoelace?"

"It's not dirty ... well, not that dirty."

The night before, he had planned to give her something. He pulled the key Dr. Gwen had given him out of his pocket, threaded it with his shoelace and then made a knot with both ends of the shoelace so the key would not come off. He didn't believe in luck, so he called it an unlock and put it around her neck.

"What is it?" she asked.

"A key," he said, waiting for some kind of sarcastic comeback. He couldn't wait to give her the same answer Dr. Gwen had given him, but it didn't have the same effect on Meri. She gave him a cold stare.

"To what?"

"Well, actually I don't know, but I call it an unlock because it's not good luck. It's a symbol to remind you that you can do anything you put your mind to."

She looked at the key closely. "What do the markings mean?"

"They mean you're gonna ace this test. Now get it done."

They were now at the entrance, and he could go no further. They shook hands and gave each other reassuring nods. She turned and disappeared into the building.

# 29: THE BLIND PATH

The test would take two hours. While the parents of the other children drove off or waited in their cars, Naz decided to investigate the grounds of International Academy. At first, he thought someone might stop him and make him leave, call security or the police to arrest him for trespassing. But just like in the neighboring town, everyone that saw him gave him a friendly nod, wave, or some other pleasant greeting.

After twenty minutes or so, Naz got bored. His shoe with no lace annoyed him as it flopped around on his foot loosely when he walked. There was a long, straight, narrow path with grass and trees on both sides in front of him. It was tranquil. He couldn't remember ever feeling so at peace with himself and the world around him. There were no human sounds, no voices, no cars, or other machinery, only the sound of the wind through the trees, the birds, the insects—the sounds of nature. He knelt down to touch the ground with his hands and take it all in.

Naz looked around to make sure no one was watching. He took off his socks and shoes. He wanted to see how far he could walk with his eyes closed, staying in the middle of the path and not straying to either side. Hiding his socks and shoes behind a big oak tree, he closed his eyes and walked slowly with his arms out imitating a mummy he had seen in an old movie. On his first attempt after about twenty steps, his bare feet found the prickly grass on the right side of the path. Naz smiled. He had discovered a way to entertain himself for the next hour or so. He tried again. This time he got a bit further but ended up jamming two of his fingers on a birch tree to his left. He cursed.

Then, Naz sat with his back against the offending tree for a while and twisted a tendril of his hair. He studied the path, and something slowly came to him, something he knew without knowing. From where he sat, Naz could see that the path veered to the right, but he couldn't see beyond that point. He stood in the middle of the path again. This time, he estimated the distance to where the path turned and the angle of the turn. Then, he closed his eyes, breathed deeply, and listened to every sound. He listened more closely than he ever remembered listening to anything before.

He imagined at the end of the turn that point that could not be seen was a place he had only ever read about: Nirvana. Then, with his eyes still closed, he walked straight down the center of the path at his normal pace with his arms slightly extended from his sides and his palms facing the sky. This time he stayed in the middle of the path. As the path turned, so did he. He used the sounds he heard and their reflections off his surroundings to guide him until something stopped him, and he opened his eyes.

There was the scent of wood chips. He looked up and saw lollipops and licorice, a playscape. *This has to be it*—all the colors, the different slides and swings.

"But she never mentioned a school; it was at a park." His heart sank for a moment, but over the last three years, disappointment was something he had gotten used to, so he shrugged it off. "And no monkey bars either, only chin-up bars."

As Naz walked around the playscape, he thought about what Meri had said earlier that morning again, about the amazing kid that could fly on the monkey bars. *Could that have been me? Well if it was, then I should be able to do this.*

Naz walked over to the highest chin-up bar. He jumped up, grabbed it with both hands, and began to swing his body forward until he went completely around the bar in circles. The third time around, his body slowed as he swung around the top of the bar. The fourth time, his body slowed even more until he stopped. He was completely still in a perfect handstand on top of the bar. After five seconds, he began to spin forward again, slowly at first, then faster and faster until on the fourth time around he let go of the bar catapulting his body into a double back somersault and landed on two feet. He stumbled backward on one foot and then turned around to look back up at the chin-up bar in amazement.

Without much thought or effort, Naz reached for the ground with both hands and immediately kicked one leg back and up and then the other, propelling himself into a perfect handstand. It was easy. He didn't wobble or strain to balance himself. It felt natural, almost as if he was standing on his feet. *Meri was right. But what else was she right about?* He wasn't willing to go any further than that. After a short while, although things in his field of vision were upside down, he didn't feel upside down anymore.

Naz stood back up and stretched out his arms and legs. They weren't tight, sore, or fatigued in any way. It just seemed like the natural thing to do. He thought about how chess came so easy to him.

"Things I know without knowing."

Naz stood on his hands again. This time, he started to laugh as he turned around a few times, spread his legs out in the shape of a V, and finished with some push-ups, never coming down from his handstand. "If only Meri could see me now." He laughed again. He walked around the entire playscape on his hands twice, but when he tried to balance on one hand, he began to falter. He stood on his feet again. He knew he could stand on one hand, but he could feel his arms getting tired. "I'm just not strong enough ... yet."

With a look of determination on his face, Naz stood on his hands a third time. This time, he closed his eyes and began to breathe deeply. He had found Nirvana in this place and was beginning to find it in his mind, too.

*I could get used to this place. There were kids bigger and older than me lined up to take that test. Maybe I could take it, too.* It never occurred to Naz until this moment the possibility of him going to International Academy. He knew he could pass the test. He could do anything he put his mind to. *Of course, then I'd probably have to do some homework.* He smiled. Naz thought about the Market Merchants. *It wouldn't work, if I couldn't work. Room and board are good and all, but what about clothes, junk food, the phones, and other stuff for Meri and me?* He lost track of time. As he drifted, he heard a noise that didn't belong and opened his eyes.

Meri and an older man were just turning the corner. Naz didn't move. He couldn't help but show off what he had discovered about himself. The man pointed to Naz and then went back in the direction in which he and Meri had come.

Meri ran over to Naz, turned her head upside down so she was seeing him close-up, face-to-face, and said, "Told you so."

# 30: WHO I AM

They took their time walking back to the train station. The trip was made complete with a stop at the hobby shop as a pre-celebration not only of Meri's self-proclaimed success on the infamous International Academy test but also a celebration of Naz's own personal discovery. At the hobby shop, they had fun taking pictures of each other with their camera phones and trying to top each other by picking what they thought was the most extravagant chess set they would buy one day when they "made it."

On the train ride back, it was Meri's turn to ask the questions. She wanted to know exactly what else Naz thought he could do. Did he know how to skate? Could he swim? What sports could he play? She reasoned that the way he ran for the Market Merchants, he had to have played some sport before, and he must've been good at it but what sport? They agreed it must've been football or track because Naz was the best at running. Meri wondered if he knew karate, how to play the piano, or speak a different language. The problem was, Naz just wasn't sure what he could do just by thinking about it. They were excited by the possibilities.

Getting up early that morning, the excitement of the day, and the pacifying ride of the Helix had Meri fast asleep within thirty minutes. Naz was left to contemplate the implications of the morning on his own.

The reality was Naz didn't know what he could do until he tried. He only knew he could walk on his hands because of what Meri had told him that morning and then he actually did it.

Naz hadn't tried to swim since coming to live in the Exclave. Just the same, he thought he could swim. But he wasn't sure if it was his imagination or something from a repressed memory, and he had done it before. The only way he could know for sure was—just like walking on his hands—to take the plunge.

He looked down at Meri as she slept on his shoulder. He missed her conversation now but resisted waking her. One thing of which he was certain, if he could speak a different language, it wasn't Spanish. He thought back to that first day of school in the Exclave when Ham had gotten stabbed.

His first Christmas in the Exclave, he remembered asking his mother for an electric piano he saw in a musical instrument catalog. Naz received an electric guitar instead. Thinking back, he wondered why she never got him the piano. It didn't cost that much more than the guitar, which he had never asked for. The guitar was OK; he liked it fine and learned how to play it by ear well enough, but he never stopped wanting the piano. On the birthday that followed that first Christmas, he asked again but still no piano. He wondered what it was about the piano that made him want it so badly, and even more importantly, why his mother didn't get it for him. Maybe it *was* just too expensive.

Naz imagined himself playing a piano. He put his fingers on his lap and thought about the piano song he always heard when the ice cream truck came down their street. He moved his fingers back and forth as if he was playing the song he heard in his head, careful not to disturb Meri. *Can I play ... or am I just pretending?* Again, he just couldn't tell if it was his imagination or something from a repressed memory. He would need a piano to find out.

There was a musical instrument store in the maze of shops and businesses they had just left, but they were miles away now. *We won't be going back there again until Meri starts school next fall.* Musical instrument stores were few and far between in the Exclave; in fact, he couldn't remember seeing one since he had moved there. But there were pianos at school—*in the music room,* and he found himself eager to get back there on Monday to test his theory.

And then there was this business of fighting. Karate, Meri said. *Could it be possible that I could have defended myself that first day of school? But I just stood there. I didn't do anything. I guess I would have needed to try at least. So what now? How do I test myself on fighting? I can't just pick a fight with somebody. I know. I could enter a contest, like in "The Karate Kid" or like Peter Parker did in "Spiderman." That's stupid. Those were just movies. If Meri's wrong, or made up some of those things she said happened at the park, I could get hurt pretty bad. But what if she was right ... about all she said, then—someone else could get hurt.*

He continued to run these thoughts and more through his head as the images outside the train transformed into the Exclave. As they passed through Marshal Park, Naz recommitted himself to his over-arching goal of getting his little sister out of what he considered a godforsaken place. Today, he saw the nicer places of the suburbs for the first time since he could remember, and his passion rekindled.

They were headed downtown to the festival. At first, it was just a reward for Meri doing well on the test. But now, there was an added incentive. The hobby shop, Meri's conversation, and a passion for chess started another fire in Naz. The last time he was at the festival was over two years ago with his mother. He had just discovered he could play chess when she pulled him away from the tables. Naz hadn't thought about it until now, but he had a score to settle: unfinished business with the Chess Master.

Word had it the Chess Master was some homeless genius that had gone mad. Almost every Saturday in the summer and fall at the Festival you could find him at the chess tables. There were nine tables arranged in a triangle with chairs on the outside of the triangle and the Chess Master in the center. The nine tables represented the nine boroughs of the Exclave. The Chess Master would only play when there were nine opponents available and no less. Some said he hadn't lost a game in over ten years. Others said he had never lost, even when he was a small boy, and that's how he went mad. Naz didn't believe any of it. He thought it was all made up, and he couldn't imagine losing to anybody, especially some homeless man.

# 31: THE FESTIVAL

Once they arrived at the festival, Meri came to life again. She thought this was the very best day of her life. She awakened that morning to a stimulating conversation and a game of chess, although she didn't win. But she could bear losing to Naz, and he was about the only one. She got to ride the Helix to another world and show what she was made of. She also got to hang out with her big brother and fantasize about the future and other amazing things.

But now she was at her favorite place in the whole world, the festival, a place where people came from all over to do almost anything. Like Naz, Meri hadn't been there in over two years, since before the accident.

There were palm-readers, face-painters, and tattoo artists. She and Naz could get on small amusement park rides, play games to win prizes, and eat different dishes and all kinds of junk food until they were sick to their stomachs. They could listen to a variety of music with live bands and singers on different stages all over the place. All of this and more were on the edge of a beautiful river where people would dock their boats and hold private parties. And then there was the circle of tents filled with art and jewelry from artisans that came from every corner of the world.

"This was Momma's favorite place to be on the planet," said Meri, as they both stood in front of one of the tents and admired the Middle Eastern sculptures.

"Yeah, but why?" asked Naz. "She never bought anything. We just went from tent to tent ... looking. Come to think of it, we didn't have any paintings or sculptures at home either."

"Maybe because of 'him.'"

"Maybe," he agreed, distracted, his attention focused on why he had come.

She turned to see what had caught his attention. "Oh," she said.

As usual, in the midst of all the tents were the nine tables in a triangle, home of the Chess Master. At each table was a chess set with a white flag next to it. The flag was either standing up, denoting that table was available for the next round or lying down, indicating it was reserved.

When Naz walked over to the tables, there were only three left. He thought it fortuitous that the table labeled Marshal Park was still available. The labels were more for show than anything else, and it didn't matter which table he reserved.

"Are you gonna play?" Meri could hardly contain herself.

Naz nodded as he put the flag down on the Marshal Park table and wrote his name on the chalkboard strips at the top and bottom of the chessboard in front of him. There was one distinguished-looking gentleman already sitting at the table across from Naz's table, but the rest of the chairs were empty. He and Naz greeted each other with a nod. It was quiet around the tables, the most peaceful place at the festival, and the Chess Master was nowhere in sight. There were only two tables available now. Naz walked away.

"Where are we going?" asked Meri.

"I wanna watch from back here." He stood near one of the tents and watched with eager anticipation, supporting his elbow with one hand and his chin with the other.

Something caught Meri's attention, and she ducked inside the tent.

"Don't go too far," he called to her. He couldn't remember ever feeling so excited, but he forced himself to remain calm. He couldn't afford to hear the voice when he was about to play the best chess player in the world—*besides me.* He laughed. As he looked on, like Meri, he couldn't help thinking this was a good day.

"*Únete a nosotros,*" said Gruff. Taking advantage of the serene moment, he had somehow managed to sneak up behind Naz undetected.

Naz almost jumped out of his skin as he turned to see what he now knew was part of a gang with designs on making him their newest member.

Mohawk and Red flanked Gruff.

Naz tried to appear calm, as he replied, "*No hablo español.*"

Gruff laughed as if he knew Naz was lying and responded, "Join us!"

"U-Um ..." stammered Naz.

"Join us or else," said Mohawk.

"But why ... why me?" asked Naz, his fear turning more to curiosity than anything.

"Let's just say, our family could use you," said Gruff. "We've seen what you do at the Market Merchants. We could use somebody on the inside."

"Well, I-I'm not really on the inside." Naz's eyes darted between the three boys.

"Plus, you and me, we're the same," said Gruff.

Naz tilted his head and squinted.

"Where's your little sister?" asked Gruff.

"She's not here. I came by myself," Naz invented, his eye giving his weak attempt at deception away.

"You're lying. I can see it in your eyes." Gruff looked at Naz intently. His eyes trailed down to find the scar on Naz's neck. "No hard feelings, right?" he said pointing to the scar. "So, what do you say? Join us."

"I ... I don't think so," stammered Naz, now worried about Meri returning.

"You misunderstand, *amigo*. We not askin'." Gruff moved closer to Naz.

"Yeah, join us or die," said Red as he moved toward Naz aggressively.

Gruff stopped Red with the palm of his hand. "Easy," he said, still looking at Naz intently. "So much hostility. You have to excuse my friend here. He's not as patient as me."

Now, up close, Naz could clearly see the symbols on Gruff's forearm. One was a sword with a serpent wrapped around it and the other, an eye. The way the symbols were shaped and designed formed the letters, IA.

"But ..." continued Gruff, "we do insist that you join us." With his free hand he began to pull out a knife, Naz assumed the same knife Gruff had used on him five weeks earlier.

Naz had no words. How could he go his own way, like Dr. Gwen said, when it didn't seem like he had a choice? Just when he knew the voice was about to return, he heard an unfamiliar but appreciated voice.

"Hello, boys," said a passing police officer. The festival was the one place near the Exclave you could find police officers in abundance. This beef-up in law enforcement was necessary to keep strong festival patronage from the suburban population.

Gruff slowly put the knife back in his pocket. He must've noticed another officer making his way to the scene. He made a motion with his hand, and the three boys walked away casually as if they were minding their own business. "We'll see you soon," Gruff finished to Naz.

Naz was so stunned by the appearance of the gang members and their boldness that when Meri returned, he didn't notice her hands behind her back.

"What?" Naz asked, clearly rattled.

"What's wrong with you?"

"N-nothing. What is it?"

"I have a surprise."

"What?" Naz asked again, still reeling.

Meri withdrew her hands from behind her back to reveal Naz's shoelace in one hand and a thin leather rope with what seemed like an unbreakable black clasp in the other. She had already threaded Naz's key.

"Perfect," he said as he slowly calmed down and put it around his neck. "Thank you. This was really starting to annoy me," he continued, pointing to his shoe.

As he finished lacing his shoe, someone tapped him from behind.

"What?" Naz jumped up as if he were shot out of a cannon, ready to defend himself.

## 32: ARTIE

Standing over Naz was one of his classmates—the round, candy-bar-eating kid from his first-hour math class and Fears' class. "Sorry," he said.

"Hey," Naz said surprised.

"What's up, Naz?" asked the boy casually as if he and Naz were best buddies. "Who are you here with?"

"My sister," Naz replied, still slightly rattled by the gang members and distracted by the tables.

The boy and Meri looked at each other.

"Excuse my brother. I'm Meri," she said, shaking his hand.

"RD," said the boy exuberantly.

"Yeah ... Meri, this is Artie," mumbled Naz.

Even though they were in two classes together, Naz had no idea what the boy's name was, and he was a little embarrassed the boy knew his name. It surprised him. After the first week of school the teachers didn't call the class roll anymore, and he couldn't remember anyone ever saying the boy's name. The boy was as invisible as Naz was. Apparently, Naz hadn't been as invisible as he had thought.

"Not Artie," the boy said. "RD ... as in Raleigh Duplessis."

"Oh ... RD," said Naz.

"Yeah, Artie," said the boy.

Naz and Meri gave each other a quick, silly look.

Naz turned his attention back to the tables as two more people, an older man and a girl about Naz's age walked over and put down the remaining two flags. *It must be his daughter.* Something resembling a dinner bell sounded, and they sat at their tables. Meanwhile, others headed over to the tables.

"I'm here with my mom and dad, and my little sister and brother, Ryan and Rodney," said Artie as he pointed back over his shoulder.

Naz looked over Artie's shoulder to see four figures. The only words that came to mind were "a matched set" as they all looked the same just in different heights, even the mother and sister. They all had curly, dark hair, only his mother and sister wore their hair longer. The smallest one, Rodney, was almost as wide as he was tall, and they were all carrying something to eat or drink.

"I'm here to see Mr. Ledbetter," said Artie. "He's gonna play the Chess Master. Did you know Mr. Ledbetter was the chess club coach at Lincoln? This is my third year in the club."

Norman Ledbetter was also their math teacher. He was an extremely friendly, middle-aged man with a nervous tick who walked with a limp. He was also a war hero who had been diagnosed with post-traumatic stress disorder and could often be seen talking to himself.

"Do you play?" asked Artie.

"A little," Naz replied, still watching as people began to take their places at the tables.

"Are you any good?" Artie looked at Naz quizzically.

"Pretty good," said Naz, modestly nodding his head.

"A little? Pretty good? He's the best," bragged Meri. "And today, he's gonna prove it by beating the Chess Master."

"Doubt it," countered Artie. "Nobody ever beats the Chess Master. The best you can ever hope for is to be the last one he beats ... or the last loser," chuckled Artie.

"We'll see," Naz said coldly.

"Raleigh!"

They turned to see a frail Mr. Ledbetter approaching.

"Now you can't even hope for that," Artie said, taunting Naz. "Hey, Mr. Ledbetter," Artie continued, eagerly shaking his teacher's hand.

"Glad to see you could make it. Ready to take some notes?" asked Mr. Ledbetter as he noticed Naz.

"Yes, sir!" said Artie. "Look who else is—"

"Andersen," said Mr. Ledbetter surprised. "What brings you to the festival this Saturday afternoon?"

"Mr. Ledbetter," nodded Naz respectfully and then he pointed to the tables. He just now noticed the Chess Master had appeared, standing silent and still in the center of the tables.

With praying hands at his chin, the Chess Master waited for everyone to be seated.

## 33: THE CHESS MASTER

The Chess Master wore a tattered tweed sport coat and a thick wool scarf, over a gray, Henley T-shirt that was missing buttons, a pair of oversized gray cargo pants that were frayed at the bottom, fingerless wool gloves, and a pair of barely worn loafers. Some of his matted coils of hair could be seen sticking through a large hole at the top of his old fedora. There was something contrived about his appearance, almost theatrical. He had a mangy beard and wore sunglasses—*probably to hide his glassy, bloodshot eyes.* Naz saw eyes like those every day on every street corner in the Exclave.

"When did he come?" Naz muttered under his breath.

"You a fan of the game, here to take some notes as well, Andersen?" asked Mr. Ledbetter.

"He's come to play," said Artie mockingly.

"Is that right?" asked Mr. Ledbetter.

Naz nodded.

"And he's gonna win, too," said Meri.

"Meri," said Naz embarrassed.

"Nothing wrong with a little confidence," said Mr. Ledbetter, smiling at Meri. "Shall we? We wouldn't want to keep the Chess Master waiting, would we?"

They all walked over to the tables, and Naz and Mr. Ledbetter took their seats.

Naz looked at the field of chess players around him. To his immediate right, making up one side of the triangle with Naz were the father and daughter. On the three tables to Naz's left, and making up another side of the triangle were an older lady, another homeless man that reeked of something awful, and some kind of nerd or bookworm that Naz affectionately termed, the Nerdsman. Making up the third and final side of the triangle were the distinguished-looking gentleman Naz had greeted earlier, Mr. Ledbetter, who was already talking to himself, and an extremely old man that must've come on the same bus as the older lady.

*No wonder the Chess Master's never lost. His competition is two senior citizens, rejects from a daddy-daughter dance, a basket case, and another homeless man. I'd be undefeated, too.* Besides himself, only the Nerdsman and the distinguished-looking gentleman could possibly have a chance. But Naz also knew oh too well from experience that looks could be deceiving.

The black chess pieces were on the outside of the tables in front of Naz and the other eight players while the white pieces were on the inside. The Chess Master would make the first moves.

The bell sounded again, and the Chess Master wasted no time. He moved to the table to the left of Naz and moved a pawn two spaces forward. Then, he continued clockwise, moving a different piece at every table until he reached the father and daughter. He had apparently made them as related, decided not to distinguish them from one another, and would play them as one until their play dictated otherwise. He smiled at them and moved his same knight on each of their boards simultaneously two spaces forward and one to the left, which seemed to confuse the father and daughter.

Finally, he got to Naz. Even though Naz couldn't see his eyes, he could feel the Chess Master looking at him through those dark glasses.

"Get 'em, Naz," said Meri.

The Chess Master turned his head slightly, apparently looking at Meri. He smiled and made what seemed like a random move of a pawn two spaces forward and then moved to his right for the second round.

Naz made his move immediately so he could watch how the Chess Master operated as well as see how the other players were doing. He figured he could tell pretty early on who would be leaving the tables first, but the Chess Master's play was erratic and unpredictable which made it hard to figure out what was going on. The Chess Master didn't seem like a master at all. He was letting weaker players off the hook when they were in obvious trouble and struggling with the stronger players. And there was something else about him, his fingers, his shoes, the way he smelled that puzzled Naz, and something even more that Naz couldn't quite work out.

By the eleventh round, the first to be seated was the first to rise as the Chess Master eliminated the distinguished-looking gentleman. The Chess Master was targeting the stronger players. Naz learned somewhere that the first rule of war was to remove the greatest threat, and the Chess Master had done that, or at least he thought he had. *Boy is he gonna be in for a big surprise.* As Naz looked at the vacant table across from him, the now standing little white flag took on a new meaning: surrender. And then there were eight.

In the very next round, the homeless man eliminated himself by passing out from inebriation. To the delight of the older lady and the Nerdsman, festival security removed him from the tables. And then there were seven.

Two rounds later, the old man's number was up and so went his flag. And then there were six.

Then, Naz heard it, the voice, faint but clear. *"Checkmate,"* the voice murmured.

Naz gave his head a little shake. He listened closely, but there was nothing. He wasn't scared, angry, or even excited anymore. His game with the Chess Master had gotten relatively boring. *I probably just imagined it.*

In the next round, the Chess Master no longer found the father and daughter team amusing, as they constantly argued with each other over which pieces to move. He took them both out of play at the same time. Someone had taught Naz that the second rule of war is that consensus is the lack of leadership, and there is no deliberation in the heat of battle, only decision, initiative, and individual achievement. And then there were four.

Naz was getting impatient. He felt like the Chess Master wasn't taking him seriously. *He hasn't taken or given anything, but neither have I. I'm playing too conservative, too passive. I need to be more aggressive.*

Then, it was Mr. Ledbetter, who had put up a valiant fight but ultimately went down in flames. There was moderate applause. He stood up, shook the Chess Master's hand, put his little white flag up and then walked over and stood behind Naz. And then there were three.

A small crowd began to gather at the tables. As predicted, the Nerdsman was giving a good account of himself, and Naz saw this as an opportunity to strike at the fully-engaged Chess Master. Naz made an aggressive move, capturing one of the Chess Master's knights. Unalarmed, the Chess Master continued his passive play with Naz, ignoring the capture with a nonchalant move of his own. *Is he still not taking me seriously?* The older lady next to Naz was decent enough but clearly no match for the Chess Master, Naz, or the Nerdsman. Yet, she was allowed to linger there with false hope.

In the next two rounds, the Nerdsman would fall, and his little white flag would rise. But he had put up a good fight. And then there were two.

And there it was again, faint but unmistakable. *"Checkmate,"* the voice said.

Naz shook his head again. *Not now.* His phone buzzed in his pocket and startled him. *Who would be sending me a text now? I told Mr. Tesla and the other Merchants I wasn't working today. It could only be … Meri.* He looked at his phone to read:

Impressive

He turned around and winked at Meri confidently. She tried to wink back as best she could. *That was a good distraction.* And the voice was gone again.

*If that last move didn't get his attention, maybe this one will.* Naz made another aggressive move, putting the Chess Master's king in check.

"Check," Naz said matter-of-factly.

The growing crowd began to mutter in awe, as this was the first time that day anyone had put the Chess Master's king in check. Seemingly unconcerned, the Chess Master quickly moved his king to safety and then moved to finally eliminate and dismiss the older lady. Dismantling the Nerdsman first and then the older lady, the Chess Master employed the first rule of war again: remove the greatest threat. He had been courteous to the older lady throughout, letting her last almost to the very end. When he finally captured her king, he tipped his hat to her, grabbed her fingers ever so delicately as she stood, and kissed the back of her hand. The older lady blushed as the now sizable crowd erupted in applause. And then there was one.

The Chess Master had orchestrated a performance, designating himself as the chief conductor. They had all been pawns put in play to carry out his sadistic show—*well, not all of us.* Naz knew there were only eight pawns on each side in a game of chess—*and all of those are gone.* Naz counted the eight now vacant tables. *So be it. Showtime it is.*

It had been well over an hour since the games began. One spectator handed the Chess Master a bottle of water. He opened the bottle and turned away from Naz to drink. At that moment,

Naz's phone buzzed again with another text. He looked at it again and read:

Most Impressive

Naz turned and looked at Meri again, this time with an agitated expression.

"What?" she asked innocently.

"You're distracting me," he responded wryly.

Someone next to Meri reached out to hand Naz a bottle of water. He declined. When he turned back around, the Chess Master was facing him, apparently staring at him through those dark glasses again. Then, the Chess Master lowered his head slightly. He was looking at something else, working something out in his head it seemed. Naz looked down. *Is it my scar?* No, it was the key hanging around Naz's neck that had caught the Chess Master's attention.

"Get 'em, Naz," said Meri.

"Yeah, get 'em, Naz," echoed a now convinced Artie.

## 34: THE MAN IN BLACK

Naz made a defensive move, trying to bait the Chess Master into a confrontation. The bell sounded, and the Chess Master stepped back from the table. A puzzled Naz looked on. Moments later a clean-cut young man dressed in a black suit appeared from the crowd of spectators and stood next to the Chess Master. *Is this fair? Is he getting help?* The Chess Master began taking off his scarf while studying the board intently. After about two minutes, with the aid of the man in black, the Chess Master used the thick wool scarf as a blindfold to cover his eyes. He intended to play the rest of the game blindfolded.

Naz's eyes panned the crowd as they murmured in awe and amazement again. *Did this impress them, this trick? It didn't mean he was good at chess.* The Chess Master memorized where the pieces were on the board. The man in black would convey Naz's moves to the Chess Master and then move the Chess Master's pieces for him. *It's a cheap parlor trick, nothing more. He's no chess master; he's a charlatan.*

Continuing to pan the crowd, Naz caught a glimpse of a familiar face. It was a face he had seen only twice before, but it was burned into his memory that first day of school. It was the face of the man who had driven by as Ham almost bled to death. And earlier that same morning he was parked in front of Miss Tracey's house. *Has he been following me ... watching me? Nah ... it's just another coincidence, only ... I don't believe in coincidences. There's too much going on. I have to focus.*

*Blindfolded!* Naz laughed. *What a joke. I should return the favor and play standing on my hands right on this table ... and the crowd would go wild.* He laughed again. *Nope, I'm just gonna beat him fair and square, no tricks.*

The Chess Master didn't take the bait on Naz's move. It was as if he were oblivious to it. He directed the man in black to carry out his next move, a basic move—*nothing special.*

Naz was insulted by the Chess Master's arrogance and passive play, so he went after him with both guns blazing. *He tried to embarrass me with his little blindfold stunt. Now I'm gonna embarrass him.* Two moves later Naz cornered the Chess Master's king again, stunning the crowd of onlookers.

"Check," Naz said arrogantly, looking at the Chess Master.

The Chess Master smiled calmly as he directed the man in black to effect his narrow escape. This infuriated Naz. He studied the board and then picked up his queen. He took aim, his target: the Chess Master's king, for the final blow. Naz would finally put this sham to shame and out of his misery for good.

"Check," Naz said triumphantly for the third and final time.

Then, without warning, it happened. The man in black took Naz's queen with the Chess Master's queen and in the process trapped Naz's king on every side. Everything fell silent. Naz looked at the Chess Master and saw his lips barely move to say along with the voice, "*Checkmate,*" and it was all over.

Suddenly, the silence was engulfed with the noise of clapping and voices, and Naz was up, shaking everyone's hand. *But I lost.* He turned back around, and the Chess Master was gone. Through all of the handshaking and accolades, Artie was saying something unintelligible while patting Naz on the back, Mr. Ledbetter was letting Naz know he would see him Monday after school for chess club, and Meri just wanted to know what had happened. Through all the commotion, his phone buzzed again. He looked at it the third time to read:

But you are not a Jedi yet.

Naz looked at Meri and thought she was rubbing it in, but he could tell when he looked at his phone that she hadn't sent him a text. She hadn't sent the previous two texts either. The sender had blocked the number, if that was even possible. Naz looked around for the mysterious man with the hat from the first day of school. He was nowhere to be found. He looked around again for the Chess Master. He too was gone. If he were looking for some excitement in his life, this day he had surely found it.

## 35: THE DARKNESS

Naz, Meri, and Artie spent the next hour celebrating Naz's success at the chess tables, even though Meri didn't quite see it that way—as a success. They continued playing games, going on the rides, and eating as much junk food as they could, just before the point of sick stomachs which was a lot of food in Artie's case. On the way home from the festival Naz and Meri's number increased by one. Artie was so enamored with Naz and his performance against the Chess Master that he fabricated an excuse to his parents to allow him to ride the Helix back to the Exclave with Meri and Naz. The excuse was something about Mr. Ledbetter requiring it for extra credit in math class and being part of the chess team.

Naz stared out of the window slightly concerned. *I hope we make it home before dark.* He had played it close, maybe too close. He wasn't exactly sure where Artie lived except that it was in Marshal Park. His biggest concern was Meri. During the twenty-five-minute ride home, Artie and Meri continued to blather on, Artie about how Naz almost beat the best chess player in the world and Meri wondering how Naz could have lost to a homeless man in the first place.

*Come on ... come on,* Naz thought as he watched the sun quickly begin to duck behind the horizon in the west. The long day of discovery and events, coupled with the drone of Meri, Artie, and other passengers, along with the hum of the Helix lulled Naz to sleep. Artie and Meri soon followed suit.

**NAZ AWOKE WITH** a start as the Helix jerked and began to slow. He wiped his eyes, looked out the window, and gasped. The sun had set, and Naz realized they had gone several miles past their stop.

"Wake up!" said Naz, nudging Artie and Meri.

They both awoke reluctantly, stretching casually and unaware of their predicament.

"We missed our stop," panicked Naz.

"Me, too," said Artie less concerned.

"What do we do now?" asked Meri.

"We have to get off ... now ... at the next stop," said Naz.

There was something else in the car ahead that Naz could plainly see in the now well-lit train. *They must've gotten on while we were asleep. First the festival, and now here, they're following me.* He cursed himself for being so careless. He had told Meri weeks before there were no such thing as coincidences, so he wasn't buying this as one either. Both Artie and Meri must've read the distress in Naz's expression as they turned to see what concerned him. It was the gang that had confronted him earlier at the festival. Naz flashed back weeks before to the sight of Red poking his finger at Tone's beak. Then, he felt the scar on his neck that Gruff had given him on the first day of school.

"What?" asked Artie and Meri in unison.

"Nothing," Naz said as he stood up. "We have to get off now!" he said, grabbing Meri by the arm and compelling her to stand.

"I'll say," said Artie, oblivious to the danger the three boys represented. "We have to catch the train coming back the other way now."

Naz was hoping it would be that easy, but when the train came to a complete stop, and the three boys in the other car stood up, he knew that he, Meri, and Artie were in trouble. He thought maybe they should stay on the train, but he was sure now the three boys would also remain on the train. He had a better chance out in the open. Naz tried to remain calm and not alert Artie and Meri to their dilemma until he could evaluate the situation and figure out something.

Naz, Meri, and Artie stepped off the train and began the walk to nowhere down the dark, deserted street. Seconds later, the gang got off the train and followed them. Under the few working lights at the station, Naz could make out Mohawk's haircut, and it made him wish, for a moment Ham were there. Even though he and Ham were not on speaking terms, Naz thought, *I could sure use his help right now.* Artie was a big boy, but he didn't necessarily spark fear in anyone who might seek to get the jump on him.

And, of course, there was Meri. *What am I going to do to protect Meri and defend myself at the same time?* Naz heard the gang laughing and speaking indistinctly in back of them. With the sun no longer out, the autumn chill took over, and Naz looked at Meri and Artie to see puffs of air expand, and disappear.

As surely as the darkness had come, as Naz anticipated, the voice returned, too "*Where are we going?*" asked the voice.

Naz remembered what Dr. Gwen had said about the voice, so he listened.

"*Where are we going?* The voice asked again and then, *"I'm scared!"*

"Why are we walking *away* from the train?" asked Artie, confused. "We need to catch it going back in the other direction."

"Fine. You go then," said Naz with a manufactured calmness as he walked forward holding Meri's hand.

Artie turned, saw the boys, and decided to continue on with Naz and Meri. There were no houses near the train stop, only abandoned businesses, condemned warehouses, vacant office buildings, and very little light.

"*Do something, Naz,*" the voice said and then, "*I'm scared,*" again.

Naz continued to listen. *That's weird. It called me by name.* That had never happened before—*and we're all scared. That's no help to me. If I'm scared, I can't do my job. I can't help Meri.*

"I'm scared," said Meri as she turned her head to see the boys behind them.

"I told you ... never be scared of nothin'," Naz said to her in a confident tone. "Plus, me and Artie are here; you got nothin' to worry about. Right, Artie?" Naz continued as he took in his surroundings.

"Right," whimpered Artie.

*Think! Think! Think! What to do? What to do?*

"It's so dark," said Meri.

*"It's too dark,"* said the voice.

"And I'm cold," said Meri.

Hearing Meri's words, Artie began to rub his hands together and then he reached down and grabbed Meri's hand.

*Dark? Embrace the darkness.* He looked over at Meri and Artie, who were also now holding hands, and realized with them at his side, there was no way he could outrun the boys. "'Embrace the darkness.' That's what Dr. Gwen said," Naz remembered and then focused on the darkness.

"Huh?" replied Artie.

Meri just looked at Naz curiously.

Suddenly, one of the rare working streetlights between the gang and Naz, Meri, and Artie blew out. Glass from the broken light rained down on the pavement, effectively slowing the gang down.

"What the ..." said Artie.

"A-A coincidence," stammered Naz.

"But you don't believe in coincidences," said Meri looking back and forth between the broken streetlight and Naz.

*That is true.* Naz took a deep breath, forced himself calm, and as Dr. Gwen had promised, the voice was gone.

"What's goin' on? What are we gonna do?" panicked Artie.

Naz ignored Artie in favor of deep thought and reflection. Meri began to pray the Lord's Prayer, and this made Naz think of Harvis' words 'To look into the skies and see an angel.' *An angel*, he thought. *If angels do exist, now would be a good time to put in an appearance.* He thought of—what he was now starting to believe was—the angel that he saw at the water fountain that first day of school when the voice said, 'What are you looking at?' *What am I looking at? What am I looking for?* And it came to him. "Mr. Fears said, 'True vision goes beyond what the eye can see.'" Naz stopped suddenly. "I know this place."

"What do you mean?" Artie asked.

"I know this place, Section 29. I lived here for two years. Artie?"

"Yeah."

"Now watch this. There's a big, old office building two blocks up and to the right. We used to play hide-and-seek there. We called it 'the maze' because of all the hallways and rooms that seemed to lead into each other. It's all boarded up except in the back ... I hope. There are two big doors that open ... kinda like barn doors but smaller."

"So?" said Artie.

"So you have to go there, ahead of us ... now!"

"What? I'm not—"

"Artie!" Naz said in a forced whisper as the gang began to close the distance between them again. "You have to go now. It's me they want, so they won't follow you. Besides, you'll need a head start. Wait for us at the doors in the back. We won't be that far behind you."

"Are you sure?" asked Artie with a desperate look on his face.

"Absolutely. Now go, before it's too late. Run!"

Artie reluctantly released Meri's hand and lumbered ahead. The gang yelled out obscenities in Spanish and English, but they didn't pursue Artie.

Meri looked back. "They're getting closer, Naz. You better do your thing."

"My thing?" He thought about all that Meri had told him earlier—about how he had handled the bully on the playground and how

Bearn had died and then he realized what she was asking him to do. "Look, Meri, there's always alternatives to violence and fighting."

He waited until he felt that Artie had a good head start. "Meri, it's your turn. Just like on our errands when I say go, I want you to run as fast as you can. Make a right at that first street, and run to the back of the building that will be directly in front of you. You'll see Artie."

"OK!"

"Firecracker," Naz said as he bent down and picked up a big rock. "GO!"

Meri darted down the street. At the same time, Naz turned around and threw the rock at the gang. Surprised, they all ducked. When they looked up, Naz was gone. He ran after Meri and Artie, and the gang followed. Naz caught up with Meri and picked her up in his arms as he rounded the building. They both found Artie waiting in agitation.

"Let's go!" said Naz as he looked down. In the moonlight, he could barely make out a woodpile of broken two-by-fours.

"I'm not going in there," said Artie. "It's pitch black. We won't be able to see *anything*."

"I'm counting on it," said Naz, as he grabbed Meri's hand and started into the vacant office building.

Artie hesitated until he heard the three boys coming around the corner. He picked up a broken two-by-four and ran in behind Naz and Meri.

# 36: INITIATE

Naz!" Artie called out in a forced whisper.

"Shhh ..." whispered Naz as he reached out and grabbed Artie's arm, causing him to jump. He pulled Artie down a hallway where Meri was waiting.

"Listen," whispered Naz. "Get on either side of me and grab my hand. Just walk slowly in the direction I lead you, and we'll be back outside in ten minutes ... ouch! And put that down before you hurt somebody," he added, grimacing as Artie had accidentally hit him in the ankle with the two-by-four.

"Sorry, but, how ... how can you see?" asked Artie, quietly putting the two-by-four down. "It's pitch-black in here. I can't even see my hand in front of my face."

"Trust me; I know what I'm doin'," assured Naz.

"Yeah, trust him," said Meri.

The gang entered the building.

"Hey, *Señor* Naz," called Gruff. "Why don't you come on out? We just wanna' talk to you."

*How do they know my name?*

"You know them?" asked Artie.

"No ... I mean ... yes," Naz stammered.

"Well, which is it?" asked Meri.

"Shut up; I have to concentrate," said Naz.

"Yeah," said Meri to Artie.

Artie tutted at Meri. Naz thought back to what he had discovered earlier at International Academy. Then, he remembered everything he knew about the vacant office building: the maze as he and his friends used to call it. It was a labyrinth of connecting hallways and offices. He would combine all that he knew about both situations, and at that moment he realized why he always came out on top in hide-and-seek when he played there. He breathed deeply and listened to every sound in the dark building.

"Yeah, Naz," said Mohawk. "Come out, come out, wherever you are ... so I can stick you and your fat friend ... like I did your other little buddy."

Naz remembered every inch of the once-familiar office building in a place he had once called home.

"Yeah, and save the little girl for me," said Red.

Naz bristled and then took deeper breaths to calm himself.

"Grab my wrists," said Naz.

Artie and Meri complied.

"Meri, start crying," directed Naz.

"What?" said Artie, surprised.

Meri started making sounds as if she were crying, and it surprised Naz even though he had requested it. He hadn't heard her cry in so long, he couldn't tell if she was faking.

"Louder," directed Naz.

Meri poured it on.

"Shut up, Meri!" Naz played along in a less convincing but adequate supporting role.

Artie listened, stunned.

"There they are. Use your lighters," ordered Gruff. "You stay here. Nobody gets out of that door," he said to Mohawk. Gruff and

Red blindly headed in the direction they thought they had heard Meri and Naz.

With his arms slightly extended from his sides and his palms facing up, Naz led Meri and Artie up and down and in and out different hallways and offices until he reached another corner of the building where he stopped them.

"Wait," whispered Naz as he continued to listen intently. "Artie, keep your eyes closed no matter what." Then Naz whispered something in Meri's ear, and there was some rustling between them.

"I can't see anything anyway. Hey! What are you guys doing?" whispered Artie.

"Shh ..." whispered Naz.

"Where are you?" yelled Gruff, frustrated.

"Over here!" yelled Naz. He was starting to enjoy himself.

"Why'd you tell 'em?" Artie whispered.

"Shh ... I got this." Naz laughed quietly. "Remember, Artie, keep your eyes closed."

"They're over there," said Red.

"C'mon," said Gruff. When he and Red could see each other through the lighter's small flames, he signaled Red to go around the opposite way so they could corner Naz, Meri, and Artie. Then, Gruff extinguished his lighter, opting for complete darkness as Naz had.

It was so dark in the building that the small flames from the lighters were not much aid to the gang, but they could hear noise coming from an area near the front of the building far away from where they had entered. They moved to investigate. They slowly converged on a small office from where the noise was coming. Just before they entered, they pulled their knives.

"Come on, Señor Naz. Join us, and nobody gets hurt," said Gruff.

As they slowly entered the room, they could see a small, dim light and hear a continuous sound coming from the center of the room. They approached cautiously and saw it was a phone—Meri's phone in the middle of the floor, her favorite song, "Love Child" playing. Angry and frustrated, the two boys cursed as Gruff stepped on the phone and smashed it to pieces.

Meanwhile, Naz had led Meri and Artie back near the exit of the building within fifty feet of where Mohawk stood guard. Naz opened his eyes so he could barely see Mohawk holding his lighter and guarding the only exit. He could also see the faint moonlight shining through the open doors. *Now we close the barn door before the horses get out.*

Meri opened her big brown eyes as far as they would stretch, as Naz had whispered for her to do moments before. Naz flashed back to the Chess Master looking at the key around his neck, and he reached up and gently touched it. Even though he didn't believe in luck, it just seemed like the thing to do. He thought about Tone and all the cool sounds he could make. *Tone would sure make this a lot easier.* Then, ever so quietly, Naz made a clicking sound with his mouth—a sound he used to make Tone fly—just loud enough for Mohawk to hear.

Mohawk turned toward the sound and slowly moved in that direction to investigate as he held the lighter in the hand of his outstretched arm. As he got closer to them, Artie began to tremble. Naz nudged Artie as he closed his own eyes and refocused on the sounds around him.

When Mohawk was within five feet, he noticed two tiny flames in front of him that grew as he moved forward. When Mohawk was inches away, he realized he was looking into a pair of eyes that reflected the lighter's flame. It was Meri's eyes. *Just a little closer,* Naz gambled. *I am the silent soldier.*

When Mohawk realized it was Meri, he smiled. "Hey, little girl," he said.

"Hi!" replied Meri cheerfully and then immediately poked him in his eyes with two fingers. Mohawk dropped the lighter, which immediately extinguished, and covered his eyes. He stood erect and screamed in agony. His scream alerted Gruff and Red, who had only just realized they'd been duped when they discovered Meri's phone. In the darkness, the two boys scrambled to Mohawk's defense, but it was too late. Naz's next reaction was instinctual and instantaneous. Mohawk was on his feet for less than a second before Naz sent him crashing to the floor with a leg sweep.

"Let's go!" Naz said as he led Meri and Artie out of the building. As he passed Mohawk writhing in pain he added, *"That ... was for my little buddy."*

Outside, Artie held the doors closed while Naz used several broken two-by-fours from the woodpile to secure the doors from the outside and effectively trap the gang members inside. Moments later, they shouted obscenities and banged on the steel doors that imprisoned them.

Naz, Meri, and Artie exchanged high fives and headed for the train.

"Thought you said there were alternatives to violence," said Meri to Naz.

"That wasn't violence. That was ... well, he was in our way," replied Naz.

"I was wondering why you let any of 'em off the hook," said Meri.

"Meri," Naz sighed heavily and shook his head.

Artie was too shaken up to participate in any discussion and walked along silently in a daze. The lights from a parked car illuminated the once dark, deserted street followed by the car suddenly pulling away. As they ran back down the street, the car that sped away struck Naz as familiar. *Why was that car here, in this abandoned place?* There were no other cars around. *Could that be the car I saw the first day of school ... the mysterious man with the hat at the chess tables earlier today? It could've been the same car ... but those headlights were so blinding in the darkness.*

*The darkness,* he laughed—*my faithful ally tonight.* He shrugged off his paranoia and took account of himself on the day's successes. He had done himself proud at the festival and protected Meri and his new friend, Artie. *Friend? I have a new friend?*

On the ride home, Naz made an anonymous call to the police and directed them to the vacant office building in Section 29 where they would find the gang.

**NAZ SPENT THE** rest of the weekend trying to explain to Meri something he didn't fully understand himself: all the things he could do and how he had lost to the Chess Master at the festival. That Sunday night he lay awake thinking about the weekend behind him, and dawn came before sleep did. *And what about the gang? What will happen to them? What did the police—who never catch anyone—do when they found them there, if they found them there? I hope that's the end of it.* He had a strong feeling that wouldn't be his last encounter with the gang. But he swore no matter what happened, he wouldn't let it haunt him anymore.

He hated to admit it, but he had fun, not just playing the Chess Master, but besting the gang as well, and all the while protecting Meri and gaining a new friend in the process. He would keep the fun part to himself when he spoke to Dr. Gwen again. *Good luck with that. I might be taking this whole "embrace the darkness" thing a little too serious.*

**NAZ LEFT MISS** Tracey's house with Meri on Monday morning free from paranoia. Their conversation on the way to her bus stop was a continuation of the two nights before. She wanted to know what Naz would do next, when and how he would try to find out more about his past and what he could do? When would he return to the festival to challenge the Chess Master again? Of course, Naz kept asking himself these same questions. The problem was he could come up with no answers.

**ON THE WALK** to Lincoln that same morning, Naz was much more relaxed and confident than he could ever remember being in the Exclave. He wasn't sure if he felt that way because he thought the trip would be gang-free or because he had discovered something new in himself that said, "I am a young lion to be feared." He paid closer attention to the derelicts that occupied the streets of Section 31. He couldn't quite put his finger on it, but there was a difference between the derelicts and the Chess Master. Maybe it was just the whipping he had taken, but he would never see them in quite the same way again. As he looked at them, he could hear the infamous voice and the words of the Chess Master blended in perfect unison, saying, *"Checkmate"* over and over again.

When he arrived at Lincoln that morning, he found news of his exploits at the festival against the Chess Master had preceded him, even though Naz had sworn Artie and Meri to secrecy about what had happened. This information undermined his whole invisibility stratagem. But Naz thought maybe it was time to step out of the shadows. In the hallways, he received everything from nods and handshakes from boys he had never even noticed or cared to know, to winks and stares from girls that he looked forward to getting to know. Like as not, he was coming into view.

In first-hour math class, Artie and Mr. Ledbetter took turns giving a play-by-play description of what occurred at the festival Saturday. Mr. Ledbetter concluded by letting the class know that Lincoln had not only found its first-ever state chess champion, but finally, the school would most likely win the chess championship he so coveted. He termed Naz a secret weapon that, right under his nose, had been indeed kept secret.

On the way to Fears' class, Naz received a text message from Dr. Gwen. Naz beamed as he read the message several times.

It's official. Our girl passed with flying colors. Tell Miss
Firecracker I said, Congratulations!!!

Ironically, Fears' class lecture was about gangs and gang violence on the streets of the Exclave. He asked his students who
among them had ever been a victim or a perpetrator of gang violence, and most of the students raised their hands. Naz and Artie
did not.

"On the first day of school, we talked ... well, I talked ... about
gangs. Does anybody remember anything I said?" Fears asked.

"That gangs are like families," blurted out Ham.

"Wrong, Mr. Martinez! Here at Lincoln, we raise our hand for
permission to speak, Son, and if memory serves, you weren't even
here the first day of school."

"Sorry, Coach," said Ham, embarrassed.

"Anybody else?" asked Fears, as he paced through the filled
rows of student desks.

As he got closer to Artie, Artie slouched down.

"Mr. Duplessis," Fears bellowed, making Artie jump and then
sit up. "Any ideas?"

Before Artie could respond Naz's hand shot up. It was the first
time he had ever raised his hand to answer a question in any class,
and when Fears called on him, it would be the first time he spoke in
Fears' class since the first day of school.

"Mr. Andersen," Fears said, his eyebrows raised in surprise.

"Exactly the opposite, Sir ... I mean, Mr. Fears, that gangs are
not our family."

Fears nodded.

Then, Harvis' hand shot up, something that also hadn't happened that year in Fears' class.

"Mr. Young," called Fears, amused.

"And that our family is at home, where we live ... with our
teachers ..." said Harvis solemnly. "And ... with our classmates."

Naz saw Harvis turn to look at him and then look away. Up to that point, Naz had never heard Harvis say a word in any class. Fears watched the two look at each other and then gave a smug laugh.

"My guys, my guys," said Fears as he picked up the morning newspaper from his desk. "I want to read something to you."

## IA: Caged!

An anonymous tip led to the capture of three notorious members of the gang simply known as IA. Police arrived on the scene to find the gang members trapped in a vacant office building in Marshal Park, Section 29. The anonymous caller gave no other information. It is unknown who caught the gang members, and they are in no way cooperating with the police.

Harvis immediately looked at Naz again. As on the first day of school, they were locked in a stare, only this time without hostility. Fears continued.

The three boys, who pled the fifth, escaped from St. Cecilia Boys' Home three months ago. They were remanded in custody of the juvenile court system, where they will await further sentencing.

Fears put the newspaper down and started clapping his huge hands in a slow rhythm. "Who are we?" he asked calmly.

Harvis stood alone and replied, "Railsplitters, Coach!" then joined in Fears' rhythmic clapping.

"A good friend once told me that true heroes don't stand in the sun with a symbol on their chest, cape flying in the breeze for all to see," Fears proclaimed as he kept clapping. "No, they prefer to use the darkness ... the shadows. They are unassuming, and they walk amongst us every day. Who are we?" he asked again, this time louder than before.

"Railsplitters!" yelled Artie as he stood with the rest of the class and joined Harvis and Fears. He looked at Naz appreciatively.

Naz shook his head slightly at Artie and then he stood up when he realized he was the only student not standing.

"True heroes aren't popular," Fears continued. "They don't hit the game-winning shot or ... kick the winning field goal, and they aren't afraid of being on the losing team if it means doing the right thing. They take a stand against all odds and the powers that be to make a difference."

Naz couldn't help but feel this message was meant for him. He felt embarrassed but at the same time proud. With all that he had gone through, he would rank this his very best day. He was starting to realize who he was and what he wanted to become: a true hero.

"Who are we?" boomed Fears.

"RAILSPLITTERS!!!" All the students gave a resounding cheer.

# EPILOGUE

## IN THE PAST...

The audience struggles and strains in vain to see on stage through the darkness Cory has created. There is the squeaking sound of a bicycle. Less than a minute later the lights go on, and Darla is at the other end of the course with all of the obstacles undisturbed.

The audience applauds. One young lady near the front of the auditorium is clapping ecstatically and waving her hand to get Cory's attention. Cory silences the crowd as he moves toward her. She stands up and shakes his hand as he puts the microphone to her mouth. He notices that she is also with child but is further along than Camille. The gentleman that sits beside her holds her other hand and looks up at her affectionately. Cory smiles as he thinks of himself and Camille.

"This is simply amazing, Dr. Andersen. Are there any significant differences in the post-performances of the control group and experimental group?" asks the young lady.

"Yes, ma'am ... and thank you. Both groups show improved performance, as predicted, but the experimental group's performance on all parameters far exceed the control group's ... and our highest expectations."

"You're welcome, Dr. Andersen." She smiles. "How so? Please, enlighten us."

Before Cory can respond, the president of the university motions for Cory to approach him.

Cory hurries over to the president and hands him the microphone.

"Yes, sir?" Cory asks.

"Tell me, Dr. Andersen, is this the type of research that our university has been funding for the past year?" asks the president.

Cory is somewhat taken aback and isn't sure what to make of the president's question. He isn't sure, but it sounded a lot like the president scolding him in the form of a rhetorical question. He decides to answer the question straightforward as he takes the microphone from the president.

"Well, yes, sir. Our research is based on the study of the mind as it applies to the human condition. We've traveled beyond the planet and divided the atom into subatomic particles. What is left but to increase our own capacity to go further? We owe at least that to those who came before us and, more importantly, those who will come after us."

Among the audience members are many scientists who are jealous of Cory's accomplishments and take the president's indictment of Cory as an opportunity to lash out and make accusations of their own. A scientist four rows in front of the president calls for the microphone. As Cory hands the scientist the microphone, a suspicious-looking gentlemen sitting next to the scientist hands Cory a card.

"Isn't this just junk science, Dr. Andersen? Come on now, psychic powers and so on, what's next telepathy, telekinesis, and clairvoyance? Really, Dr. Andersen," says the scientist.

Cory is visibly rattled. "Maybe!" says Cory, brusquely. "But I'll tell you what is junk science: creating useless models based on the work of geniuses like Einstein, Curie, Freud, Pavlov, Watson and Crick. It's derivative drivel without an ounce of innovation."

The president stands up and begins to make his way out of the auditorium, and this fires up Cory even more.

"We pat ourselves on the back and pass out awards every year, for what?" asks Cory angrily as he looks over to see Camille peeking out from the stage wing, biting her fingernails nervously. "People are starving because we're not smart enough to feed the planet. People are dying by the millions from sickness and disease that we're not intelligent enough to eradicate. The solution lies within us, but we have to make ourselves smarter. And that's where it starts," Cory finishes passionately as he points to the stage where Darla is still sitting on the bicycle.

A student yells from the back of the auditorium, "You tell 'em, Dr. Andersen."

A few more students chime in, "Yeah ... Yeah ... Yeah!"

A fringe group of protesters calling themselves Apocalgreen sees this as an opportunity to forward their agenda and starts chanting, "No more experiments! No more experiments! No more experiments!"

University security converges on the situation as a shoving match begins. Pandemonium ensues. People throw things onto the stage. Darla screams and runs. Camille snatches her up and ducks back into the wing of the stage.

**IN THE CAB** ride home, Cory and Camille are silent. Cory looks straight ahead, but in his peripheral vision, he can see Camille staring out of the window and angrily shredding a tissue the master of ceremonies had given her. In his hand, Cory notices the card the suspicious-looking gentleman had given him. He reads it for the first time.

I'll fund your research. Give me a call!

Cory turns the card over to read:

Wintersal Neurological Institute
Avander Pauling
312.838.1931

# THANK YOU

Did you enjoy the book?
You can make a huge difference.

Positive reviews are powerful agents that make my books stand out.

Honest reviews put my books on a level playing field with other books in my genre and make it easier for my other books to find you in the future.

Constructive reviews are a form of feedback and reciprocity between the reader and writer that helps shape future creative processes.

In other words, I'll continue to write the books you like, and you'll continue to like the books I write.

So, if you've enjoyed this book, I would be grateful if you could spend a few minutes leaving a review (it can be as short as you like) on the book's Amazon page.

# APPENDIX
## IA: W.O.W.

Dr. Gwen's 50 Words of Wisdom Every Student
That Takes a Standardized Test Should Know

| WORD | PAGE | WORD | PAGE |
|---|---|---|---|
| Contrast | 7 | Estimated | 20, 149 |
| Demonstrate | 28, 53 | Show | 24, 28, 73, 144, 151, 157, 168, 189 |
| Examine | 84, 100 | Choose | 77 |
| Retell | 41 | Define | 8, 63, 145 |
| Compare | 10 | Sequence | 63 |
| Interpret | 63 | Order | 7 |
| Develop | 132 | Predict | 131, 141 |
| Plan | 50, 84, 85, 90 | Assess | 16 |
| Support | 69, 79, 82, 157, 180 | Prioritize | 77 |
| Preceeded | 141 | Constant | 8, 91, 117 |
| Summarize | 145 | Decide | 59 |
| Categorize | 144 | Conduct | 77 |
| Extended | 104, 149, 181 | Solve | 71, 131 |
| Infer | 72 | Explain | 13, 73, 82, 88, 121, 132, 184 |
| Hypothesize | 145 | Transformed | 136, 154 |
| Convince | 16, 43, 82, 134 | Opinion | 75, 114 |
| Solution | 32, 81, 191 | Prove | 34, 162 |
| Defend | 160, 175 | Fact | 28, 29, 68, 73, 91, 139, 154 |
| Effect | 79, 124, 147, 171 | State | 145 |

Continued on next page.

| WORD | PAGE |
| --- | --- |
| Reflect | 141, 182 |
| Judge | 27 |
| Evaluate | 175 |
| Rank | 188 |
| Distinguish | 165 |
| Classify | 107 |
| Select | 102 |
| Combine | 180 |
| Relate | 30 |
| Organize | 100 |
| Identify | 107 |
| Construct | 107 |

# MERI'S WORD SEARCH PUZZLE

```
S W O H S Y N V T C E L E S
E M A U V Y E D I C E D G H
Q X C O N T R A S T X M Y R
U K A E W D E V E L O P E C
E M Z M U L L K J H O F H A
N D P U I Z O U D T L O T E
C E X R P N D I H E O E V T
E F N L O G E E C S T A E R
Y I A R E V S T E A L J F O
V N Z E Y I E K R U O E D P
X E I L S Z K O A H T E O P
L B D A X W B T E A Z H C U
W K T T S A E Z T I U M K S
P X W E L N I S R V R G W H
T O L E G R Q O R D E R F U
C C C N A Q G S O L V E T E
A C L M U E E U B N D N X B
F E M A T R Y Z O A A T E N
F U F A S D I I I T E N M O
S Q C F N S T L S N I B K I
A A K E E U I N D B A N N N
C U F A L C O F M Y A G M I
T E B O Y C T O Y R S G R P
D W S A E P C C Z I Q D B O
```

| | | | |
|---|---|---|---|
| Contrast | Evaluate | Summarize | Prove |
| Reflect | Develop | Rank | Solve |
| Solution | Choose | Categorize | State |
| Judge | Plan | Classify | Opinion |
| Examine | Define | Extend | Combine |
| Defend | Support | Select | Relate |
| Effect | Sequence | Constant | Organize |
| Fact | Elaborate | Decide | |
| Show | Order | Hypothesis | |

# MERI'S CROSSWORD PUZZLE #1

## Across

5. to carry out, manage, or control something

6. to examine two or more things in order to discover similarities and differences

9. to say what is going to happen in the future

11. to be aware of the difference between two or more things

13. to make an approximate calculation of something

14. to examine something in order to judge it

15. to tell something again, especially in a different form

## Down

1. to build or assemble something by putting together separate parts in an ordered way

2. to explain, describe, or show how something works

3. a change as a direct result of action by something else

4. to conclude something on the basis of evidence or reasoning

7. to order things according to their importance

8. to recognize something and be able to say what it is

10. to explain the meaning or significance of something

12. to change

13. to inspect or study something in detail

# MERI'S CROSSWORD PUZZLE #2

## Across

3. to offer support for something, especially by arguing against something else

6. to assign to classes or groups

8. something that can be shown to be true, to exist, or have happened

9. to find the answer to a question or puzzle

11. to broaden or expand the range, influence, or scope of something

13. to think seriously, carefully, and relatively calmly

15. the view somebody takes about a certain issue, especially when based solely on personal judgment

16. to arrange items in the sequence in which they are to be dealt with

17. to decide which of a number of things is best or most suitable

## Down

1. to assess the quality of something or estimate possibilities

2. to work out in advance and in some detail how a thing will be done

4. to consider or examine something in order to judge its value, quality, importance, extent, or condition

5. to establish the truth or existence of something by providing evidence or argument

7. to explain, demonstrate, or prove something in a logical way

10. to give an account of something with enough clarity and detail to be understood by someone else

12. to make a choice or come to a conclusion about something

14. to make somebody sure or certain of something

# MERI'S CROSSWORD PUZZLE #1
## ANSWER KEY

| Across | Down |
|--------|------|
| 5. Conduct | 1. Construct |
| 6. Compare | 2. Demonstrate |
| 9. Predict | 3. Effect |
| 11. Distinguish | 4. Infer |
| 13. Estimate | 7. Prioritize |
| 14. Assess | 8. Identify |
| 15. Retell | 10. Interpret |
| 12. Transform | |
| 13. Examine | |

# MERI'S CROSSWORD PUZZLE #2
## ANSWER KEY

| Across | Down |
|--------|------|
| 3. Defend | 1. Judge |
| 6. Classify | 2. Plan |
| 8. Fact | 4. Evaluate |
| 9. Solve | 5. Prove |
| 11. Extend | 7. Show |
| 13. Reflect | 10. Explain |
| 15. Opinion | 12. Decide |
| 16. Order | 14. Convince |
| 17. Choose | |

# GET TWO FREE SONGS
## FROM THE IA SOUNDTRACK
## AND EXCLUSIVE IA MATERIAL.

The best thing about writing is building a relationship with you, the reader. I occasionally send newsletters with details on new releases, special offers and other pieces of information relating to the IA series and my other projects in the works.

And if you sign up to the mailing list, I'll send you:

1. A copy of the song Journey by John Darryl Winston II.
2. A copy of the song Gone by John Darryl Winston II.
3. And an official IA fact sheet containing stats and facts about the compelling characters of IA.

You get two songs and the official IA fact sheet, FOR FREE, by signing up at my website: www.johndarrylwinston.com.

## ABOUT THE AUTHOR

John Darryl Winston is a graduate of the
Motion Picture Institute of Michigan, the
Recording Institute of Detroit, and Wayne
State University. He also holds an MFA in
Creative Writing from Wilkes University. He is
an educator, coach, musician, and songwriter,
but considers himself an author first—mainly
because he believes that miracles and dreams
live in the written word. He lives in Michigan
with his daughter Marquette and intends to
acquire an African Grey parrot one day when
he conquers his irrational fear of birds.

CPSIA information can be obtained
at www.ICGtesting.com
Printed in the USA
BVOW08s1211150218
508094BV00001B/95/P